# Praise for *Mr Wigg*

'Inga Simpson gives readers a character so realistic . . .
that it's hard to believe he's a creation of fiction'
*Herald Sun*

'a tender story'
*Country Style*

'a contemplative story that will touch your heart'
*Marie Claire UK*

'resonantly powerful at every bite . . . Just beautiful.'
*The Australian Women's Weekly*

'Beautifully crafted and brimming with warmth.'
*Who Weekly*

'*Mr Wigg* captivates to the end.'
*Good Reading*

'a sense of what is right and good about the world over-
whelmed me on closing this book.'
*Books+Publishing*

'captures the pleasures of a simple country life'
*Vogue*

ALSO BY INGA SIMPSON

*Nest*
*Where the Trees Were*
*Understory*

# MR WIGG

## INGA SIMPSON

hachette
AUSTRALIA

**Queensland Government**

*Mr Wigg* has been written with the encouragement of the Queensland Writers Centre (QWC). Inga Simpson participated in the 2011 QWC/Hachette Australia Manuscript Development Program, which received funding from the Queensland Government through Arts Queensland.

**hachette**
AUSTRALIA

First published in Australia and New Zealand in 2013
by Hachette Australia
(an imprint of Hachette Australia Pty Limited)
Level 17, 207 Kent Street, Sydney NSW 2000
www.hachette.com.au

This edition published in 2017

10 9 8 7 6 5 4 3 2 1

National Library of Australia
Cataloguing-in-Publication data:

Simpson, Inga.
Mr Wigg/Inga Simpson.

978 0 7336 3784 1 (pbk.)

Older people – New South Wales – Fiction.
Families – New South Wales – Fiction.
Country life – New South Wales – Fiction.

A823.4

Cover design by Ellie Exarchos
Cover images: iStock and Shutterstock
Author photograph courtesy of Claire Plush
Text design by Ellie Exarchos
Typeset in Granjon LT Std by Bookhouse
Printed and bound in Australia by McPherson's Printing Group

MIX
Paper from
responsible sources
FSC® C001695

The paper this book is printed on is certified against the Forest Stewardship Council® Standards. McPherson's Printing Group holds FSC® chain of custody certification SA-COC-005379. FSC® promotes environmentally responsible, socially beneficial and economically viable management of the world's forests.

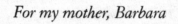

*For my mother, Barbara*

*The nectarine and curious peach,*
*Into my hands themselves do reach;*
*Stumbling on melons, as I pass,*
*Ensnared with flowers, I fall on grass.*

'Thoughts in a Garden', Andrew Marvell (1621–1678)

# Summer

# Orchard

**M**r Wigg had squandered his life. That's what his son thought. Probably others thought it, too, and maybe they were right. He was neither wealthy nor famous, and the great swathe of property his family once owned had been split up between brothers and sons. He was alone now, which people thought was sad, but he was too old to remarry and lacked the heart.

He leaned on the front verandah railing while the sun came up over the hill, washing everything pink. A moment of tenderness before the heat began to build. Birdsong rushed to fill the space the night left behind. The way Mr Wigg saw it, he'd had a pretty good life: built a home, raised a family. Young folk, who haven't lived through a war, are slow to learn there's more to it all than tearing round and round the paddocks trying to make money.

He slid on his hat, which drooped so much around the edges now it limited his field of vision, and stepped down into the garden. There was a little moisture on the grass, enough to dampen the toes of his boots. He wandered through each of the standard rose circles that formed the centrepiece for the front garden, breathing in their perfume. They weren't what they used to be. Although they still bloomed, the colours were subdued, their size diminished. He managed the pruning, fertilising, watering, and so on – after all, they were not unlike fruit trees with their hips and flowers – but the roses had been his wife's domain.

It would have been the same if she had been the one left behind; the peaches would have sulked, refusing to give their best. Some of the other trees' little quirks would have escaped her and they'd have started acting up. Answers to problems that arose – scale or collar rot or fruit failing to set – would not have been immediately apparent, requiring belated consultation of books and other growers.

They had had their separate worlds; hers the roses and flowerbeds, the sunken garden and hedges. She had insisted on pruning those bloody hedges herself, by hand, until she was no longer able to grip the clippers.

The lawns, the orchard and most of the vegetable patch were his. She had learned years ago not to interfere or comment, but accept the resulting fruits with praise, just as he had learned to stand back and admire her rare blooms. His wife did not complain about daily armfuls of oversized zucchini but found new ways to cook and preserve them. After all, it was all good food and should not go to waste.

Some days they would go off to work after breakfast and not see one another until lunch, although only a cooee apart. They would not enter each other's space unless invited, especially when major work was in progress. As they aged, this occasionally had unfortunate consequences. His wife had lain in the sunken garden for several hours, her arm pinned under a log she had been trying to move from the retaining wall. 'I knew you would come,' she had said, quite calm.

Mr Wigg had fallen from his ladder and called out 'Help!' – with no response. He'd had to drag himself eight hundred yards through the dirt and around to the rose garden, with what turned out to be a fractured tibia, only to find her singing along to the radio.

Mr Wigg's orchard was backlit by the low-angled sun, his trees gilt-edged. The grass along the fence was a little long but not yet browned off. It was coming up to that time of year when the trees offered up their reward for the year's hard labour. The peaches and apricots were bending with fruit, only a few weeks off ripe, and Mr Wigg had already begun plucking off a handful of mulberries as he went past.

The first mouthful of each tree's fruit held the flavour of the soil, the rain, the air and all of the glorious variables of the four seasons of a particular year. At his age, when you couldn't afford to look too far ahead, every year's harvest was a gift. That perfect moment, when he held the weight of the fruit in his hand and raised it to his mouth, somehow still contained all of the expectations of the world.

# Mulberries

Mr Wigg worked his way around the circumference of the tree, climbing up and down the ladder. The mulberry's heart-shaped leaves scratched his face as he worked, but it was cool in their shade and he soon filled the ice-cream container with ripe berries.

They had planted the mulberry when they were first married, nearly sixty years ago now, as the cornerstone of the orchard. Its dark branches extended over the chook yard, dropping ripe fruit for the hens to peck up. It had also spread to spill fruit on the path around to the house, which had made his wife cross every year. He had hosed the stains away each evening to appease her but there were just as many there again the next morning. Now he left the berries where they lay.

The kids used to climb right up to the top of the tree, disappearing into the leaves, to fetch the darkest and fattest fruit. They would return with purple fingers, mouths and feet, like wild creatures, and compare their catch. His wife would cook up a batch of mulberry pies, and churn mulberry ice-cream, and they'd know summer was really upon them.

'All right,' she would say, serving up seconds, 'since we're having such a purple patch.' And their son and daughter would giggle over each other at the table, silly with sugar.

Time had passed slowly in those days. They hadn't been able to imagine the children growing up and moving away, beginning lives of their own.

Mr Wigg popped a particularly fat, dark, berry in his mouth. 'Good crop this year, Mr Mulberry.'

There was, of course, no reply. It would be fair to say that the mulberry tree was a bit aloof. He was physically set apart from the others – position always determined so much about a tree – and their youthful boasting didn't interest him much. They might have sought advice from one who had grown for much longer, seen many more seasons, but that is the way of the young, thinking they know it all. The mulberry, too, might have shared his rumbling thoughts on the meaning of bearing fruit year after year, or stories of some of the remarkable things he had seen. Instead he stayed silent, having learned that younger trees lacked the patience to listen.

Mr Wigg left the ladder where it was for tomorrow and took his container inside, scraping his boots off on the back step. The cracks and lines of his hands were deep purple, and he'd managed to squash a berry into the peak of his hat.

He washed up in the laundry, wiping his hands on the scrap of old towel he kept hanging by the sink. It was already hot on the verandah, with a haze building outside. He popped the berries in the fridge and poured himself a glass of cold cordial.

All that thinking about mulberry ice-cream had him fancying a bowl or two. It was too hot to do anything much outside until later, and the churner was still in the pantry somewhere. He gathered together an armload of cream and eggs headed to the kitchen.

Mr Wigg drove in shrinking circles around the back lawn singing 'Close to You' at the top of his lungs, though birds were more inclined to suddenly disappear when he mowed. When he sang, too, for that matter. Late afternoon shadows stretched across the cropped buffalo grass behind him.

They had bought the ride-on when he broke his leg, so his wife could do the mowing. Although she had managed easily, she had been all too happy to give it up again when the leg mended. Cut grass always made her sneeze.

The mower was a marvellous machine, key start and far more manoeuvrable than his old tractor. It even had a roof you could attach to keep off the sun. He lined up his tyres in the last lap's tracks, sailing around and around as he had so many times before. It was never monotonous in the way of ploughing the paddocks, or the dry, itching task of harvest. His son said he put all his energy in the wrong places, but you had to follow what you enjoyed to some extent.

Mr Wigg had built a little wagon he could attach to the mower to carry prunings and fertiliser: a gardener's dream. It was fun, too, for pulling the grandkids around in, though they had told him his son did not approve. Worried about his driving, he supposed.

With a satisfying last *vroom*, he cut the centre out of his lawn circle and lifted the blades. He shifted into top gear and sped down through the open door of the shed to park the machine with a screech.

The sun was setting over yellowing paddocks. He wandered closer to the fence to take a look. The crop was drying off nicely, thick and tall. He unchained the gate, pushed in a few steps, up to his waist in wheat. He snapped off a hairy head to rub between his hands, bent to blow away the chaff, and cradle the grains. Bit one between his teeth. They were good and full, high in protein.

He hadn't managed to get a top crop off the hundred acres since before the children were born. Things had picked up a little when he and his son had still been running the place – his son had put a lot of work into improving the soil during his first few years – but nothing like this.

Mr Wigg sighed and let the grains drop into the dust. They leased these last paddocks to the neighbours, the O'Briens, for a bit of income: bringing in more in rent than he had ever made cropping them. Those O'Brien boys – a father and his three sons – knew what they were doing, and worked hard. Good people, too. The whole district respected them, didn't begrudge them a single dollar.

They put his own efforts to shame. 'Real farmers,' his son always said, as if he should have been born into that family. His son had given the O'Briens first option on his farm, but they hadn't been able to get the finance, some problem with the deeds to one of their places.

If he had worked harder, been a better farmer – and father – things might have all turned out differently, but there was no use wishing for what was already gone. Mr Wigg hooked the chain back around the post and over the bolt and made his way back up to the house.

# Strawberries
and Cream

**M**r Wigg opened the oven door for little Lachlan and helped him slide the cake tin onto the middle shelf.

'Okay, so now we need to set the timer,' he said. 'How long did the recipe say?'

'Twenty-five minutes,' Lachlan said. He set about turning the dial around, tongue poking out the corner of his mouth.

'Very good.'

'That's a long time.' Fiona was sitting on the stool, licking cake mixture from the spatula.

'Long enough to pick some strawberries and whip some cream.'

'Bags picking the strawberries,' Lachlan said. His t-shirt, tie-dyed in pink and red, had him looking rather like a squashed strawberry already.

Fiona frowned. 'You always get to pick things.'

'Do not.'

'We can all pick them together,' said Mr Wigg. He lifted Fiona down from the stool, transferred the spatula to the sink, and wiped her mouth and hands with a damp towel. 'To the strawberry patch!'

Lachlan ran ahead and grabbed an ice-cream container from the pantry. Fiona leapt off the back step and ran after him, her denim flares flapping.

The children applied the 'one for me, one for the bucket' rule very seriously, counting out loud as they plucked off fruit. Mr Wigg followed, picking what they missed from beneath the leaves.

'They're real good this year, Poppy,' Lachlan said.

'Thank you.' Mr Wigg smiled. 'It must have been all that sheep manure you two brought me.' They had bagged it up from under the shearing shed for pocket money. Lachlan's idea, apparently, but Fiona had been willing, armed with her mother's gardening gloves. It was more than he'd ever managed to convince his own children to do when they were small. They had turned up their noses at anything with too much aroma.

Fiona stopped at the end of a row, staring up at the scarecrow as if caught in its gaze. Mr Wigg had used one of his wife's old blouses this year, something a bit brighter to try to keep the pesky starlings away.

'Do you miss Grandma?' she said.

'I sure do.'

'Mummy said she died of a broken heart.'

Lachlan threw a strawberry, which barely missed his sister's head. 'Fiona!'

She turned, a strand of blonde hair wisping across her face. 'What?'

Lachlan frowned and shook his head.

'Your grandmother died of cancer,' Mr Wigg said. 'She was sick for a long time.'

'Oh,' Fiona said.

'I think we have plenty of strawberries now,' Mr Wigg said. 'Who's going to help me whip the cream?'

Mr Wigg washed up while Lachlan dried and Fiona put away what she could reach. The cake cooled on the wire rack.

'Smells *good*,' she said. 'It makes me hungry.'

'Not long now, sweetie.'

Lachlan hung up the tea towel. 'Did you grow strawberries up at the old farm, Poppy?'

'Sure did,' he said. 'The vegetable gardens were out the back of the kitchen and the strawberry patch was right down the bottom, near the road. One time, the cook sent me down to pick the strawberries, only about Fiona's age I would have been, when a big team of drovers came along. They were pushing a mixed herd of cattle, horses and . . . ostriches!'

Fiona and Lachlan giggled. '*Poppy.*'

Mr Wigg shrugged. 'It's true,' he said. 'There must have been two hundred of them, black and white as a newspaper, with their long necks bobbing along like this.' He stuck his head out and tucked it in.

'Don't we have emus, not ostriches?' Lachlan said.

'Yes, but ladies used to wear ostrich plumes in their hats; it was all the rage,' Mr Wigg said. 'So someone must have been farming them. Anyway, the horses and cattle were acting like it was any other day, and the ostriches were just walking alongside them. They all seemed to be getting along rather well, actually. Chatting about the weather and so on. But one of them fixed its beady eyes on my basket of strawberries and I didn't dare move. They are quite big close up. Or they seemed so when I was your size, anyway.'

'Why didn't they fly away?' Fiona said.

Lachlan laughed. 'Ostriches can't fly, stupid. They run.'

'I knew that,' she said.

'Which is faster, Poppy, a horse or an ostrich?' Lachlan said.

'Huh. That would be close, I think. Maybe an ostrich,' he said. 'Unless it was a racehorse.'

'Then why didn't they run away?' Fiona said.

'That is a very good question.' Mr Wigg drained the sink and put the rest of the dishes away. 'And I don't know the answer, I'm afraid. Perhaps they were on invisible leashes,' he said. 'Lachlan, you can hull the strawberries, then slice each one in half.' He handed Fiona a clean spatula. 'You can put on the cream.'

'Yay,' she said.

Mr Wigg lifted the sponge onto its side and gently cut it in half with the bread knife. He placed the bottom half on a white plate, cut side up, and the other back on the rack. 'Off you go,' he said.

Fiona spread the cream over the cake, wielding the spatula like a trowel. Mr Wigg helped her even it out right to the edges. She lifted the spatula towards her mouth.

'Ah! Don't lick it yet,' he said. 'We've still got to put more on top.'

Lachlan placed the strawberries, one at a time, until it was evenly covered.

'Very good.' Mr Wigg lowered the other cake half, the cream gluing it down. 'And now we just do the same again,' he said. 'Only neater.' He spread the cream and then stood back. 'You probably don't remember, but your grandmother made a mean sponge cake. She preferred to use passionfruit instead of strawberries though.'

'I think strawberries look better,' Lachlan said. He and Fiona took turns placing strawberries around the cake's edge.

Mr Wigg smiled. 'Let's see how it tastes.' He cut three large slices, transferred them to plates and handed out forks. They sat at the kitchen table, chewing and nodding. 'What do you think?'

'Yum!' they said in perfect time.

'It's lovely and light,' Mr Wigg said. 'Not bad at all.'

'Thank you, Poppy,' Lachlan said.

The three of them put their forks down and sighed. Fiona picked at the crumbs around her plate. 'I love cooking,' she said.

'Eating, you mean,' Lachlan said.

Mr Wigg heard the front gate and got up.

'Daddy!' Fiona climbed off her chair and ran to the back door. 'We made sponge cake!'

'So I see.' He wiped a smear of cream from her nose.

'They did most of it themselves,' Mr Wigg said.

'Really? Maybe they can start doing the cooking at home.'

Lachlan and Fiona pulled the same 'like that's going to happen' face and Mr Wigg sneaked them a wink.

'You have to try some,' Fiona said.

'We've got to keep going, love,' Mr Wigg's son said. 'There's someone coming back to have another look at the place.'

Fiona's head dropped.

Mr Wigg put the rest of the cake in a Tupperware container and pressed on the lid. He'd seen the red ute, with its black and white South Australian plates, nosing around the day before, which had given him a strange feeling in his stomach.

'C'mon,' Lachlan said. 'Dad can have some for dessert tonight.'

'A second look, you say?' Mr Wigg handed over the container.

'I'm pretty sure they're going to make an offer. They want to put in a vineyard.'

'Grapes? Well . . .' Mr Wigg wiggled his toes over the edge of the step, yellow nails curling over their ends again already.

His son sighed. 'I just want it over now, Dad,' he said. 'C'mon, kids.'

# Peaches

Mr Wigg leaned in the shade of the water tank, arm above his head, admiring his white peach trees: Bendigo Beauties. And beauties they were. Of the three, one had always grown a little larger, in a classic vase shape. Its trunk was dead straight and it held its rough-barked branches out like the strong arms of a friend.

You could prune a tree, influence how it grew, but its own strength and character always played a part. It was genetics, going right back down the line to the first graft.

A cloud wisped over the sun. There was a bit of a build up in the west but not enough to come to anything at this time of year. He'd seen the red ute drive out again today, around morning tea time, so figured there had been a shaking of hands. He hadn't been able to stomach his own tea, despite an extra teaspoon of sugar and a ginger nut biscuit to dunk in it. The milk was fine; it was him that was all curdled. It wasn't as if the place was his anymore anyway, but passing out of the family altogether was something he would rather not have lived to see.

Mr Wigg scuffed across the furrows to inspect his peaches, protected by curved leaves drooping in rich, even green. A red blush crept over their cream skin; if the rain held off for another week or so he would have a near perfect crop.

The yellow peach trees behind him had already started up. It had been a mistake to plant them so close together, thinking they'd keep each other company. Now he couldn't admire the whites without the yellows getting jealous and vice versa. It was funny how those most similar always seemed to have more trouble getting along.

He nursed the weight of a yellow peach in his hand. 'Magnificent,' he said. 'Not long now.' The yellow peach trees stood a little taller, and stopped whispering insults to the whites. But they all knew the white peach was his favourite fruit. The yellow flesh was much more practical, able to be bucketed inside without bruising and cooked in all manner of ways.

The white was a sensitive creature, easily marked and bruised but brimming with juice and ambrosial flavour. They were best eaten straight from the tree, or, as he had discovered, carried one or two at a time to the privacy of the kitchen. Devouring the pale-fleshed fruit – and showing any sign of pleasure, which was difficult to avoid with sweet juice dripping down your chin – in sight of the other trees incited them to nasty insults about colour and clingstone.

The white peach trees were as delicate as their fruit, their branches would droop, their leaves would curl inwards, and if he didn't step in – with a stroke to the trunk and reassuring words – they'd begin to drop their fruit, one at a time, onto the hard ground.

That night he dreamt of a whole orchard of white peaches, acres of vase-shaped trees heavy with velveted globes. The soil was russet brown, recently turned over. On top of a soft hill, one particularly magnificent peach presided over the others. Its branches came together in a twisted circle, suggestive of a crown.

The Peach King could see the weather coming from far away and would whisper warnings down the rows to the others, giving them the chance to set themselves against the wind or open their leaves to rain.

When the locust plague came one spring – a terrible screeching swarm consuming anything green in its path – the sky grew dark, and the peaches, flush with tasty spring growth, trembled and whimpered. The Peach King called up an answering cloud of birds to meet the locusts head on, feasting on those who had already feasted enough. And the orchard was saved.

There were stories that the Peach King was a magic tree, older than time. Others said he had once been a great man, ruling over fertile lands and gentle people with a beautiful queen. Whatever the whispers, he was one of them now;

his fruit – though a little larger and sweeter – formed just as theirs did.

At dusk they sang in the season. The sun set red behind the Peach King, light fading on the orchard until only his silhouette remained.

Mr Wigg woke early, the image of the tree still with him. He hurried to get dressed, pulling yesterday's clothes up off the floor. The magpies were warbling away but the sun was not yet up.

He slid on his boots at the back step and walked out to the orchard in half-light. He squinted at the trees, their leaves rustling; everything was just as he had left it. He smiled. 'Just as well, I suppose. I couldn't very well look after any more of you.'

Mr Wigg stopped in front of one of the lemons and fumbled with his zipper. His stream arced feebly and then dribbled away, like everything else he had watched diminish. As a young man, he had taken many things for granted, including his capacity to urinate.

The lemons suffered the indignity, knowing it made for better fruit. For some reason, the other trees seldom raised the issue these days; only the persimmon dared spit 'toilet tree' when in a rage. Perhaps they felt embarrassed for an old man, worried he was drying up.

He switched over the tap at the tank, turning the trees' drippers off and the back hose on, and set to watering his melons by hand. The day raced to begin, the light changing as he moved along the row. He bent, now and then, to pinch off any wizened shoots, or a melon that had shot out from the extremities only to wither and die on the vine.

He turned off the tap and gathered a handful of strawberries on his way to the chook yard, reaching down for the tin by the gate. His ladies chattered around his legs, picking at the grain he scattered. They had had a productive night; he had already half-filled the tin with lightly speckled eggs. Mrs Wigg had insisted on giving the chooks movie star names over the years: Scarlett, Brigitte, Marilyn, Sophia, Ingrid, Katharine and so on. It had made things a bit difficult when the family had sat down to eat one of them for Sunday lunch. Mrs Wigg would sniff and wipe her eyes all through the cooking of 'poor Vivien', and the children would look doubtfully at the crisp golden skin of the pet they had fed or chased around only the night before, torn between watering mouths and broken hearts.

In the kitchen, two of today's eggs went straight into a batter as Mr Wigg made delicate pancakes, flipping them in the air with a flourish. He set himself up at the table on the back verandah with lemon, sugar and sliced strawberries and went back for the teapot.

Over a second cup of tea, he turned over a new page in the notebook Mrs Wigg had given him last birthday and took the draftsman's pencil from his top pocket. He began a rough sketch of the Peach King, trying to remember the exact details of his shape.

# Seventh Test
# Batch

**M**r Wigg worked in the kitchen with the fan on flat out and the radio beside him. The seventh Ashes Test was starting in Sydney and Australia's new captain, Ian Chappell, had won the toss and sent the Poms in to bat.

The third Test at New Year's had been a washout, abandoned without a ball being bowled. Four matches in the series had been drawn, the only win going to the Poms. This extra Test match, the first in history, was a chance to level the series, although England had already retained the Ashes. Still, Boring Boycott was out injured, and the new Australian bloke, Lillee, was setting the place on fire, so there was every chance of salvaging some pride.

Mr Wigg used a hot mat to open the stove door and threw in another piece of wood. The temperature gauge on the verandah indicated a hundred-plus day but it was far hotter in the kitchen. His son kept saying he should get rid of the wood stove and buy an electric one. And an electric hot water system. Reckoned it was *insane* cutting wood to keep the stove going to heat the water in the height of summer. He'd miss it in winter though, and the electric oven wouldn't be as good for bread or baking. Not everything that was new was better.

His son wouldn't be coming around as much, he supposed, now his place was sold. Though they had still to find a new farm to go to. He'd miss the company, and the help. If there was an upside, it would be that his son would be far too busy for a while to think of all the reasons why Mr Wigg should move into town.

The pot of water had come to the boil. Mr Wigg lowered in a yellow peach with an egg spoon and counted out forty seconds before placing it in the bowl of iced water. He slipped off its skin in one movement, throwing it in the bucket for the chooks, like a crumpled coat. He repeated the process until lines of naked peaches covered the bench, glistening and vulnerable as newborns.

Edrich, replacing Boycott at the top of the order, was off to a slow start and Luckhurst was looking luck*less*, yet to score. Dougy Walters came in to bowl, fielders crowding all around and Luckhurst was GONE for a duck. One for five.

Mr Wigg smiled as he sliced each peach in half, slipped out the stone and cut them in half again. There was something about beating the Englishman at his own game. He popped the occasional peach quarter in his mouth, savouring the tart sweetness.

By the end of the batch, there was juice running over the edge of the breadboard onto the bench and down the front of the cupboard door. He licked his fingers and wiped his hands on his apron.

Edrich and his new partner, Fletcher, were hanging on, cautious against young Lillee, and O'Keeffe never gave too many runs away. If the Australians could keep up this pressure, another wicket would fall. The commentators were going on about the sacking of the previous captain, Lawry, despite his good form. A captain had to take responsibility for the team's performance, he supposed, and losing the Ashes *was* a national tragedy, but it seemed a bit pointless to get rid of one of your best batsmen for the last match of the series.

Mr Wigg bent down to pull the boiler out of the cupboard, used the bench to pull himself back up. The pot was old and full of dings but still did the job. Not that he wouldn't like one of those fancy new electric Vacola kits. Only took seventy minutes, apparently, and no need for thermometers and the like. Coming out of the first war, and before the days of refrigeration, Fowler's preservation system had revolutionised Australian kitchens. Not a bad effort for an Englishman.

Fletcher cracked a four over mid-wicket, dragging the commentators' attention back to the match. One for twenty-eight and drinks. Mr Wigg practised the shot with the wooden spoon. There was nothing like the sound of leather on willow, especially when it was you who had played a top shot. When you knew it was good right off the bat and didn't bother running, just watched it fly to the boundary.

Mr Wigg threw a couple of peaches into a saucepan with sugar and water. You could just use water with the jars, but the syrup produced a richer result. Outside, the lawn was bleached white, heat haze rising off the path. Not a bird in sight. They would be in the shade somewhere, beaks open. He stirred the syrup mixture a little, waited for it to come to the boil. Fletcher came back from drinks still thirsty and hit another four; he was putting Edrich to shame, already overtaking his score.

Mr Wigg rinsed out his wide-necked Fowler jars, dried them and placed them on the bench. He packed peach quarters into each jar, leaving as little air as possible, before moving on to the next: his own little production line.

Edrich was finally out, after more than two hours, for a meagre thirty, leaving England at two for sixty. Mr Wigg poured syrup into the jars, stopping about an inch from the top. One jar was left a little short; he'd eat those first.

Mr Wigg dropped the saucepan in the sink, licked spilled syrup from his hand, and set the rubber rings on the jars' necks. It took longer than it should have, his hands shaking too much to line them up. The lids were more cooperative, and he secured them with their shrugging shoulder-shaped clips.

He filled the boiler with water and set it on the stovetop, stopping to hear Fletcher go, caught Stackpole, bowled Dell.

He placed the jars into the water, one by one: individual pressure cookers.

'Dolly' D'Oliveira was next in. Poor bloke hadn't been out of the news since making the team. Born in South Africa, he was a fine all-rounder but couldn't play in his own national team because he was of mixed race – in this day and age. So he'd had to move to England.

Mr Wigg popped on the boiler lid and rummaged around in the third drawer for the thermometer. The jars needed to heat up to 98 degrees over an hour to be properly cooked and sterilised.

Dolly took a single to get off the mark, earning him generous applause. Despite good form, he hadn't been selected for England's tour of South Africa, the British cricket board pandering to the South African Government, the press reckoned. Then, at the last minute, one of the squad – Cartwright from memory – had to pull out and the selectors called in Dolly to replace him. Well, then it was all on. The Prime Minister of South Africa opposed Dolly's selection. And, in protest, England cancelled the tour.

BOWLED. Dell had knocked down Dolly's stumps. Four for sixty-nine and lunch. The poor bloke's luck wasn't improving.

Mr Wigg sat down at the table to write labels for his peaches. He had contemplated calling them 'Seventh Test Peaches' but that probably wouldn't mean anything to anyone else. He might even forget himself in a year or two. 'February, 1971' was dull but no doubt more practical.

Mrs Wigg hadn't been able to abide cricket. She feigned not to understand the rules and ranted about how much time he wasted listening to it; that was before the days of televised matches. Mostly he had it on while he was doing other work, so her objections had seemed a little unfair. In later years she had sometimes done her knitting and so on in front of the television. 'To keep you company,' she said. Funnily enough, her interest in doing so appeared to peak when young O'Keeffe was bowling. He cut a pretty fine figure in his whites.

Mr Wigg checked the water temperature, slid the boiler off the hottest part of the stove, and left the lid off. He set about cleaning up. Somehow, he had managed to get peach syrup and juice on just about every surface.

By the time he had finished mopping the floor, the players were due back from lunch. Mr Wigg cut two thick pieces of fresh bread, buttered them, and sliced one of the tomatoes he had picked only this morning. He sprinkled over a little salt and fetched a beer from the second fridge, poured it into a glass and carried it and his plate into the lounge room.

The sudden cool goosebumped his forearms. He turned on the television and fiddled with the picture, getting it right just in time to see Hampshire go, caught Marsh, bowled Lillee, which had a certain ring to it. Five for ninety-eight. Mr Wigg set himself up in front of the air conditioner to enjoy the rest of the day's play.

# Snow and Harvest

**M**r Wigg turned the teapot three times before pouring. When no one was around, which was most of the time, he liked to use his wife's old cup and saucer. She used to collect the things, each one a different pattern and shape with matching cake plates; they were all still on display in the sideboard. This was the only one she had ever used, though, unless she put on an afternoon tea. Its delicate pink rose and winding green stem had pleased her.

He couldn't even get a finger into the handle, had to hold it between his thumb and two fingers like a giant. Or an oaf, more like it. He could drain the cup in a mouthful, too, but had learned to sip more slowly and refill it several times.

The peaches were good with his Weetbix. Smooth, easy to cut with the spoon, and the perfect balance of sweet and tart. He took his time, although he needed to get all the morning's jobs done before the cricket started. England had collapsed to be all out for a hundred and eighty-four. This had put the Australians in late in the day, though, and they lost Eastwood for five. Today's first session would set up the rest of the match.

He put the open jar of peaches back in the fridge, and took the clips off the others, popping them away in the drawer in a tangle. He carried the jars, three at a time, into the pantry. He used the step ladder to climb up and place them on the second top shelf, next to what was left of last year's and the year before's. There were a couple left from the year before that, too, their juice clouding now. He climbed down and put the ladder away, wiped the film of sweat from his face with his hanky.

He washed up in tepid water – having let the stove go out overnight – glancing out the window at the wisps of high cloud against a bright blue sky. It was meant to be another scorcher with a chance of a late change; that chance looked to be a slim one. Nonetheless, he should pick any ripe fruit in case it came to something.

This time, the pantry light blew with a *fizzt* as he flicked the switch. 'Bugger.' He stood in the doorway until his eyes adjusted and rummaged around for the pile of ice-cream buckets, knocking something off onto the floor with a clatter. Whatever it was could wait. He collected his hat and gloves on the way outside.

Mr Wigg sat in his blue vinyl recliner, legs up, nursing a bowl of peaches and ice-cream, spoon paused halfway to his open mouth. The English fast bowler, Snow, had just struck the Australian batsman, Jenner, on the head with a bouncer, laying him out flat on the ground.

'They should wear helmets.'

Mr Wigg turned at his son's voice, a drip of melted ice-cream slipping off his spoon onto his shirt. 'Well, if they're going to bowl balls like *that*.' He popped the spoon in his mouth, swallowing the smooth sweetness.

'Nice and cool in here,' his son said, sitting on the arm of the lounge.

Mr Wigg nodded. Jenner was up but leaving the field. RETIRED HURT. The crowd was on its feet. The umpire appeared to be giving Snow a warning, signalling chest height and shaking his head, but the English captain, Illingworth, had something to say, too. When Snow returned to the boundary at fine leg, an angry member of the crowd leaned out and grabbed at his shirt, starting a scuffle.

Mr Wigg's son laughed. 'I thought this was meant to be the gentleman's game?'

Play stopped. The English captain was leading his team off the field, protesting against the Australian crowd's behaviour.

'Ridiculous,' Mr Wigg said, running his hand through what was left of his hair. He spooned up the last of his dessert and put the bowl down on the floor.

'They're not called whingeing Poms for nothing.'

Mr Wigg looked at the clock. 'You finished harvest already?'

'Header's broken,' he said. 'Belt. Can't get another one until tomorrow afternoon.'

'Much to go?'

'Down to the last five hundred acres but –'

'I don't reckon it'll rain,' Mr Wigg said. 'Doesn't feel like it will. You'll be right.'

'Hope so,' he said. 'Looks pretty good. Maybe a hundred bucks a ton if we can get it in.' Illingworth was leading the English back onto the ground, the crowd booing them all the way. 'Well, that was a monumental waste of time.'

That was what his son said about a lot of things. 'Shame they didn't stay off; they would have forfeited the match,' Mr Wigg said. 'Probably the only way we can win from here. Would you like a drink? Since you've knocked off.'

His son got up. 'I'll get it.'

Long-haired Lillee was out there batting with Chappell, one wicket in hand – unless poor old Jenner came back, his jaw was broken, they said – with a lead of just fifty runs. They'd need much more than that to win on this pitch.

'You've got that fridge way too cold, Dad. There's no head on the beer.'

Mr Wigg shrugged. 'I like it cold in the summer,' he said.

His son shook his head, sighed, and held out the glass. 'Lachlan said something about them reducing it down to a one-day match?'

'That was just a one-off, because of the washed out Test in Melbourne,' Mr Wigg said. 'Something for the crowd.

32

They've been playing a few of those at state level, but I can't see it catching on.'

His son nodded. Nursed his beer. 'You know we've been looking at the Thompson place, out on old Emu Creek Road.'

Mr Wigg stretched out his legs, sending a splosh of beer out of the glass and onto his shorts. 'Yes.'

'Well, they've accepted our offer.'

Mr Wigg blinked.

'We can move in at the end of the month.' His son gulped at his beer. 'You know, since the place is empty.'

'It's not too small?'

'It's what we can afford. With what the bank will lend us,' his son said. 'The Traubners take possession at the end of the month. It gives us a few days grace to move everything and get the place cleaned up here.'

Mr Wigg nodded, sipped his beer. Traubner? What sort of a name was that? The patterns in the carpet blurred and spun.

'Dad?'

Mr Wigg tried to focus on his son. 'That's good, then,' he said.

'I can still come out every week. To see you.'

The crowd was cheering again. The Australians must have done something good.

'You'll have your hands full enough for a while. Don't worry about me.'

# Apricots

The cool change overnight had allowed for a better sleep, which he'd needed. There hadn't been much rain with it, just a light shower to freshen things up. Hopefully his son had got the rest of the wheat off before sundown. A good last harvest would be a big help. Mr Wigg picked apricots from the top of his old wooden ladder, breathing in their perfume. The tree's rounded leaves fluttered in the breeze, tickling his face. The fruit were a good size this year, a comfortable fit in the palm of his hand, and their skin much smoother than his own. The colour was good, too, bright orange with a pink blush where the cheek caught the sun. No marks or spots.

He split one open for closer examination: luscious and velvety, softer around the base of the smooth dark seed. Flawless. He popped one half into his mouth: juicy and sweet with a sharper finish. He flicked the seed out from the other half with his thumbnail and chewed it slowly while he continued to pluck off fruit with an upward twist.

The apricot was one of the oldest trees in the orchard, planted when they built the house. It had been their first fruit produced, too, a modest harvest eaten straight from the tree when it was not yet as tall as his wife. In later years, they had picnicked in its shade, admired its pink blossom in spring, and spent days together in the kitchen cooking and preserving its fruit. Apricots were his wife's favourite.

This had been no surprise to Mr Wigg, although he had never said so – he was pretty sure it wasn't the sort of thing you could say to a woman – because when he had first seen her little bottom, that evening in their dimly lit bedroom, its shape had reminded him of an apricot.

Apricots and peaches were also distantly related to roses: a point of intersection for their garden passions. In those days, he had been relegated to jam duty. His first few attempts weren't that flash, either, ending up too runny or too dark. She would just click her tongue and tell him where he had gone wrong. Usually several times. They ate it all anyway; every year. Even his mistakes were better than store-bought jam.

When his blue plastic bucket was full, Mr Wigg climbed down, steadying himself with a hand on the tree's sturdy trunk, to fetch another. He filled four buckets in all, leaving at least one more behind; the fruit inside the tree's own shade needed another day or so.

The apricot stood a little taller, the weight it had been carrying much reduced, and pride in the results of another year's work sending its sap surging.

Mr Wigg sampled another, even larger apricot, and sucked on its seed, its three ridges sharp against his tongue. Apricot seed kernels had been used to treat tumours since ancient times. Their oil contained amygdalin, or vitamin B17, which liked to attack cancer cells. Not that the ancients could have known that, but somehow they figured out it was useful. Mind you, the body also turned amygdalin into cyanide, so too many kernels could be lethal.

After his wife's diagnosis, Mr Wigg had kidded her into having a handful of raw kernels each day. Cyanide seemed no worse than all the other chemicals they were pumping into her by that stage. Not that any of it made any difference in the end. It had reached a point where she was resigned to go. 'I'm so sick of being sick,' she'd say, or, 'I can't go on.' He'd begged her to keep fighting, tried to convince her of all there was to live for. It wasn't as if he had wanted her to suffer; he just hadn't been strong enough to let her go.

How were you supposed to live without someone after fifty-odd years? The thought had seemed worse than death at the time, still did some nights, when he lay awake staring into the dark, but here he was all the same. Life had a way of going on whether you were interested or not, and then you found yourself taking pleasure in a few small things, and a few more.

He had felt guilty at first, enjoying a single blossom without her, until he'd realised he wouldn't have wanted her feeling like that, if things were reversed. Life was for living, while you had the chance, like a marriage; you had to cherish each day.

Mr Wigg halved and pitted apricots the rest of the morning, with all the windows open and the radio up loud. Things were not going well in the cricket. Chasing two hundred and eighty-odd in their second innings, the Australians started badly, losing Eastwood on the sixth ball without scoring a run. Only stubborn Stackpole had put up much resistance, whacking the ball around the boundaries until Snow knocked over his stumps on sixty-seven. The day's real highlight was in the fifth over, when Snow broke his hand fielding a ball on the boundary fence, earning him his biggest cheer of the tour. A fair exchange for breaking Jenner's jaw. Even without him, the English had had Australia on the ropes at the end of the day's play: five for a hundred and twenty-three.

Today, young Greg Chappell, playing in his sixth match, offered the only real hope. Mr Wigg started the first batch of stewed apricots, measuring out two pounds of fruit with the old scales, two cups of sugar, and placing the lid on the boiler. He set the timer; these days, especially with the cricket on, he was inclined to lose track of time.

He was still preparing the jars when Chappell was GONE for thirty. Mr Wigg sighed. Seven for a hundred and forty-two; it was hopeless.

He checked the simmering apricots, touching one gently with the edge of the spoon. Perfect. Mrs Wigg would have been pleased. He took them off the heat just before the timer went. It was important not to overcook them; they were best when firm enough to retain their shape. How they looked in the jar was half the battle when trying to impress the show judges. Not that he intended entering; they'd given up years ago after winning every category several times over. What were they supposed to do with all those ribbons? He'd made a showcase for the back verandah, out of ironbark and glass. When it was full, he and Mrs Wigg had called it a day.

He filled the jars with hot apricots, admiring their colour and breathing in the steam. The little bit left over – less than a third of a jar – he scraped into a bowl for his dessert.

Mr Wigg wasn't sure about all these flashy new blokes in the cricket team, with their gold chains and talk about getting paid for playing. Representing your country should be honour enough, and surely experience still had to count for something. The decision to dump Lawry, for a start, was looking pretty silly right now.

He washed up the boiler and started a double batch of jam, adding sugar and a little pectin to the mountain of fruit. By the time he'd given it a good stir and moved the boiler onto lower heat, Australia were ALL OUT for a hundred and sixty. 'Bloody hell.' A disappointing end to a disappointing series. If they couldn't win a single match at home, how could they hope to win in England next time? There wasn't much to feel good about.

The sun was breaking through outside. A crow called from the clothesline. Mr Wigg turned the radio off, sick of the commentators' post-mortem, and washed up, stopping to stir the jam and test its consistency over the back of the old wooden spoon. Years of jam making had cured it to the same rich brown as a wet apricot kernel.

# Bottles and Jars

**M**r Wigg had just cut himself a slice of cold watermelon when the electrician turned up. The young bloke, Scott, had taken over from Mal, who had done all the original wiring in the place. Mal had kept coming out when they needed him, even after he retired, but he was up in the nursing home now. Said he would've liked to leave the business to a son, but since he had four lovely daughters instead, he'd had to sell.

'Morning, Mr Wigg,' Scott said.

Mr Wigg shook his hand and let him in. 'How's business?'

'Can't complain,' he said. 'Problems with a light, was it?'

'In the pantry. I changed the bulb but it's still not working. It went with a bit of a fizz, so I'm thinking a wire's gone.'

'Through here, is it?'

Mr Wigg nodded.

Scott put his tools down and shone his torch up at the ceiling. A smoky brown mark radiated out from the base of the light fitting. 'Ah,' he said. 'I'll just pop out and get the ladder.'

Mr Wigg didn't know whether to eat his melon, offer the fellow some, or wait till he was gone. Mal would've had some with him once the job was done. Caught up.

The house lights went off. The young bloke had remembered where the power box was. It was odd the way power made a sound when stopped, a kind of jolting lurch. Life leaving the body, though, was silent. When his wife died, there had been no warning, no sound, the way you'd expect when someone was leaving for good.

Mr Wigg stood out in the hall while Scott eased the ladder through the doorway. He watched him unscrew the fitting, letting it dangle from the ceiling. Scott inspected the wires and then shone the torch around inside the ceiling cavity. 'You got rats?'

Mr Wigg shrugged. 'There's probably a few up there.'

'One of 'em has had a munch on the wires back here, eaten it nearly through. Then it burned out, I reckon. I'll just splice a new piece in?'

'Sure.'

Scott gripped the new wire in his mouth and took a pair of pliers from his toolbox. 'All this wiring is getting pretty old, Mr Wigg.'

Mr Wigg nodded. 'Most of it would be fifty-odd. Except the sleep-out. It's a bit more recent.'

Scott looked at him, probably assessing which would go first, him or the wires. 'I don't have to do it today, but it would probably be a good idea to check it all over,' he said. 'If it's fine, we'll leave it alone but I wouldn't want a fire starting up there on you.'

Mr Wigg thought of his watermelon growing warm on the sink. 'Next time?' he said. 'I wouldn't mind an extra power point out on the verandah, too.'

'No worries,' he said. 'Want to turn the power back on for me?'

Mr Wigg followed the hall out to the verandah, running his hand along the wall in front of him and feeling for the step with his feet. When he returned, Scott was grinning. The pantry's bottles and jars were lit up in various shades of orange and red and yellow.

'You stocking up in case of some sort of famine?'

Mr Wigg leaned on the shelf dedicated to chutneys and relishes: pear, fig, peach, tomato, and quince; little treasures each one of them. 'That's exactly what my son says.'

He said quite a lot worse, actually. That he was hoarding food that nobody would ever eat. Or still cooking for four when it was just him. It seemed silly now, he supposed, with a supermarket in town and everything available all year round. But you never knew what lay ahead. He and his wife had eaten well through two wars and the Depression thanks to his orchard and pantry, and fed many others. There had been drought years, too, when some of the trees did not produce, and they had to rely on what was bottled. The kids didn't seem to remember that. 'What's your favourite fruit?' he said.

'Probably peaches,' Scott said.

Mr Wigg smiled. 'See that shelf behind you, second from the top? Take a jar from there.'

'You don't have to do that, Mr Wigg.'

'As you can see, I have plenty. You'd be doing me a favour.'

'Thank you,' he said. 'My wife would kill for peach trees like yours. We don't have much space in our little yard.'

'My wife preferred apricots,' Mr Wigg said. 'Though she enjoyed her peaches as well.'

'I might have to drop a few hints for a crumble, like her mother makes.'

Mr Wigg beamed. 'Peach crumble? That would be splendid. Take another one, there you go. A jar each.'

# Gold Dust

**M**r Wigg held the back door open. Lachlan's face was puffy and Fiona's ponytails were askew. His son, whose own hair could've benefited from a brush, handed over their bags. 'I think that's everything. It's a bit crazy at home.'

Fiona's mouth, which until now had been in a firm pout, opened with a wail. 'All our things are in *boxes*, Poppy!'

'We'll have your rooms set up for you at the new place on Sunday night, possum,' Mr Wigg's son said.

'I don't *want* a new room. I like my old room.'

'Fiona, we've talked about this.'

'And I'm not leaving Po-p-p-p-py.' All those p's came out either side of a little sob.

'We don't want to go, Dad,' Lachlan said.

'Come on now,' Mr Wigg said. 'Let's get you inside.'

He carried Fiona into the kitchen and sat her on her stool. Lachlan slouched in after them, and leaned against his sister.

'Sorry,' his son said, rubbing his forehead. 'I don't think they really understood until we packed.'

'They'll calm down soon enough. Go on, I know you've got plenty to do.'

'I'll be back around five on Sunday.'

Mr Wigg nodded.

His son turned the corner at the end of the path, head down.

Mr Wigg's kitchen, meanwhile, was a picture of despair. Both children were sniffing and he'd forgotten to put another bit of wood on the fire. Not a great start. 'Right then, who wants a cup of cocoa?'

They nodded as one, their little mouths turned down.

He slid the kettle over and stoked up the fire. 'We're still going to see a lot of each other, you know. You can visit in the holidays and we'll cook up a storm.'

Lachlan and Fiona exchanged a look. 'It won't be the same,' Lachlan said.

'Some things will be different. But it will always be the same between us.' He handed Fiona his hanky and set to work mixing cocoa and sugar into a paste with a little milk while the kettle came to a boil.

Mr Wigg eased himself onto a kitchen chair and blew over the edge of his cup. Lachlan and Fiona copied him, nursing their Bunnykins mugs. Just as his son and daughter had on sad days. 'I thought we'd make steamed apricot pudding to have tonight.'

Half-hearted nods.

'What about a story, Poppy?' Lachlan said.

'Have I told you the one about your great-great-grandfather having to travel in disguise during the great gold rush?'

They shook their heads.

'Well, my grandfather – your great-great-grandfather – bought and sold gold. Miners came into the general store and sold him their gold. Then he would ride to town on his horse, with his saddlebags full of gold.' Mr Wigg sipped his cocoa. Fiona had stopped crying, and made an attempt to blow her nose in his big hanky.

'But going regularly like that was a bit dangerous. Can you think why?'

'People might want to steal it,' Lachlan said.

'I was thinking of some people in particular.'

Lachlan frowned.

'Robbers!' Fiona said.

'Yes. Do you remember going to a cave out the back of the mountains with your mum and dad?'

'Ben Hall's cave!' Lachlan said. 'He was worried about bushrangers.'

'That's right. People were held up all the time on the road, for their money and watches and gold. The district Gold Commissioner himself had been shot in an attack on a stage coach. So he travelled at different times, on different days. And sometimes he wore a fake moustache, and different hats, or glasses and a beard.'

'Did he use different horses, too?'

'He did. That's very clever, Lachlan. Perhaps you take after him a little.'

Lachlan smiled.

'And he always carried a revolver under his coat. Just in case.'

Fiona put her mug down on the bench. 'What's a revover?'

'A *revolver*, is . . .' he gestured to Lachlan.

'It's a gun,' Lachlan said. 'Like cowboys use.' He made a draw and shoot action.

Mr Wigg smiled. 'That's right. A hand gun with six rounds. Luckily your great-great-grandfather never had to use it. He got that gold to the bank every time.'

Fiona's mouth lifted a little.

'I still have it in the cabinet in the lounge room. Would you like to take a look before we start cooking?'

Fiona slid off the stool and took hold of his hand, following just behind him through the glass door.

Mr Wigg leaned down to open the lounge room cabinet.

'You can hold it if you like. It doesn't work anymore.'

Lachlan held the revolver out flat at first but then wrapped his hand around the grip. 'Was it like the wild west, Poppy?'

'A bit. Gold tends to make people a little crazy, no matter where they are.'

'Now see this here, this old book. It's a ledger, with all the gold bought and sold from the shop written here. In my grandfather's writing.'

'I can't read it!' Fiona said.

'That's because you can't read,' Lachlan said. He had the benefit of a three-year head start, which he was inclined to rub in more often than necessary.

'Can too. The writing is all loopy.'

Lachlan rolled his eyes. '*You're* loopy.'

'Do you want to get those scales out, Fiona. That's how he weighed the gold. That's it. Careful now.'

She set them on the carpet between them. Peering into the bowls as if she might find some leftover treasure.

Mr Wigg tapped the book. 'That's all the different amounts that came in. What he paid for it. And who he bought it from.'

Lachlan ran his finger down the columns. 'How much is an ounce?'

'Of gold?' Mr Wigg held his fingers about half an inch apart. 'About that square.'

Fiona dragged the ledger closer, flicking back to the front pages.

'What's that in the cover there, Fiona? That lump.'

Fiona slid her fingers under the leather and wriggled at it. She held it out in the palm of her hand.

'Well, will you look at that!' Mr Wigg said. 'It's an ounce of gold.'

'*Poppy!*'

'It's true,' he said. 'Look at the way it sparkles. C'mon, let's weigh it.'

Fiona dropped it onto the scales, tongue out, and Lachlan helped her balance them. 'It's just under,' he said. 'How much is it worth?'

'A couple of hundred dollars.'

'We're rich!' Lachlan said.

Fiona frowned. 'Did you put that there, Poppy?'

'I'd forgotten about it,' he said. 'Your grandmother found it when she was first going through the ledgers years ago,' he said. 'Someone must have tucked it away for a rainy day.'

'But it's not even raining,' said Fiona. At this, the pair of them collapsed into giggles on the floor.

Fiona shovelled mashed potato into her mouth, eager to clear her plate for once, on the promise of dessert.

'Was great-great-grandfather rich, Poppy? With all that gold.'

'He was well off for a time. He also had a number of stores and pubs, which were very busy during the gold rush.'

Lachlan sliced his roast chicken into bite-sized pieces. 'What happened?'

Mr Wigg put down his knife and fork. 'The gold rush ended, as booms always do. He used the money to buy up land and started farming.' He got up to fetch the crumble from the oven. Lachlan cleared their plates. 'Can you reach the ice-cream, Fiona?'

'Yes.' She leapt from her chair, negotiating the door and skidding to the fridge and back in a blonde blur. Fiona mushed her ice-cream into the crumble. 'Delicious.'

Lachlan rolled his eyes. 'Tell us again about the tunnels.'

'Well, the mine was called Seven Mile. It was a whole network of mine shafts. And some of them joined up.

Grown men could walk upright, for more than seven miles underground. And it was all lit up with lanterns.'

'Did you go down there, Poppy?'

'I was too little. Like you,' Mr Wigg said. 'The mine had closed down by the time I was old enough.' He chewed his mouthful of crumble, which was rather good if he did say so himself. 'You know, they never filled all those tunnels in. When I was first married, the doctor at the time – Perrera, I think he was called – was driving along Loaders Lane, not far from where the main mine shaft was, during a wet winter and the ground gave way right in front of him. The car started to disappear, headfirst, and he had to climb out over the back seat.'

Lachlan's spoon was waving, empty, in the air.

'He stood by the edge of the hole and watched his whole car vanish into the earth.'

'Did they get it out?'

'Nope.'

Lachlan frowned. 'Is there any gold left, do you think?'

'Maybe a few bits and pieces were missed. But there were a lot of people looking very hard for a long time.' He scraped up the last of his crumble. 'Though there is a rumour that old Mr Armstrong buried a jar of gold sovereigns out the back of his place, which used to be a school.'

'Sovereigns?'

'They're gold coins. Worth a lot of money now. Me and my brothers used to look for them, digging holes all over the place after school. And I'm sure we weren't the only ones.'

'And no one has found them yet?'

Mr Wigg shook his head. 'It's only a rumour, mind.'

'Have you brushed your teeth properly?'

'Yes, Poppy.'

'What about you, MisChief?'

'Yes!' Fiona tilted up her head and peeled back her lips.

'Right. Into bed then.' He tucked Fiona's sheets and blankets across her tightly the way she liked it. Though she'd soon wriggle it all loose.

Lachlan had propped himself up against his pillows. 'You didn't bring a book, Poppy.'

Mr Wigg covered a yawn. 'I thought you'd be all worn out and tired of stories.'

'Never,' Lachlan said.

Mr Wigg sat on the end of Fiona's bed and moved his slippered feet in circles to try to get some circulation going. 'Have I told you about the Peach King?'

They shook their heads.

'Once upon a time there was a Peach King. He ruled over fields of peach trees as far as you could see in every direction. Perhaps you can picture him, in winter, a big old gnarly tree, bare-trunked, silhouetted on his hill against a fading sky.

'The trees were entering their dormancy, which is a delicate time. So, to help them settle down, he told them – with a great booming voice carrying across the acres – a story about a wild peach seedling that had aspired to grow in the grounds of a great white palace. It had never seen the palace but dreamt of it often, and knew it to be real.

'It had grown straight and true, and practised, every day, bowing as deeply as it could in case a palace official chanced to ride by. It whispered praises to the queen and imagined her eating its fruit. The seedling began to hear tales of a magnificent orchard tended by a magical gardener, conjuring up fruits the size of melons. It longed to be chosen to live among those trees.

'A bent old man came walking through the woods one cool afternoon, whistling a wicked song about fair maidens and firesides. The peach seedling had been dozing, and tried to straighten itself. The man smelled of fertile earth and bletting fruit. He drank from the stream by which the seedling grew. The seedling found itself desperate to please the man, despite his uncourtly attire and wizened hands. But it had yet to produce its first fruit and its autumn leaves were almost gone. All it could think of was to try to sing.' Mr Wigg looked at Fiona, hand by his ear, as if listening.

'La la lala la,' she said, giggling.

Mr Wigg smiled and shook his head. 'The old man, however, was rather deaf and could not make out the words. He peered at the little seedling, head tilted, but kept on his way. His whistling faded off into the distance.

'It was a long winter for the seedling. It dreamt of golden halls, and silver platters of fruit dripping with sweet juice that it would provide for the queen and her courtiers.

'When spring came, the seedling shot up and out, budded, and finally bloomed. Its pink blossom lit up the woods. It realised then, with a sudden shrinking of sap, it was alone. There was no other peach with which to share its spring joy.'

'Oh,' Fiona said.

'Just then, two lovers ran into the woods, he chasing she. The young man snapped off a sprig of blossom and presented it to the beautiful maiden. The peach seedling sang.'

This time, Fiona was ready. '*Oh what a beautiful morning . . .*'

'That's more like it,' Mr Wigg said. 'The next day, the old man returned, seeking the source of the blossom he had found on his daughter's dressing table. The seedling heard him whistling along the path. The queen's gardener – for that's who he was, of course – stopped and stared at the seedling, now a young peach tree in glorious flower. "What art thou, oh, beauty?"

'The seedling was too nervous to sing, and could only manage to hum, beginning a vibration in its heartwood that quivered out to its twigs.

'This time, the queen's gardener heard the music, tickling his ears like a child's laughter. "Wouldst thou bloom for the queen?"

'The seedling couldn't reply, it was so swollen with pride and hope. But it knew somehow all its dreams were going to come true.'

Fiona had fallen asleep. Mr Wigg kissed her forehead. 'We'd better leave it there, then.' He eased himself off the bed, and shuffled across the room to Lachlan, legs stiff.

'Poppy?'

'Yes, Lachey?'

'I don't want to move.'

'I know, love,' he said. 'I'm sorry.'

'Mum says it's all Auntie Deb's fault.'

Mr Wigg coughed. Pictured himself blocking a fast, swinging ball with the full face of the bat. 'Well, it's not quite that simple,' he said. 'We've all had to make some difficult decisions.'

Lachlan clung on to him. 'I wish we were still rich. Like in the olden days.'

Mr Wigg brushed the boy's hair from his face. 'Money isn't everything, son. Or property. It's the people we love that make us happy,' he said. 'You'll have a great time exploring the new farm. And everything will be just the same whenever you visit here.'

Lachlan let out a breath too big for such a small body.

'Goodnight, now.'

'Night, Poppy.'

# Grapes

**M**r Wigg leaned on the corner post of his orchard, watching the paddocks burn. He had imagined it all being Lachlan's one day, or maybe even Fiona's; she seemed to have some sort of affinity with the natural world. Life, of course, seldom works out the way you imagine. He should have learned that by now.

The three hundred acres was already black, the stubble burnt away and ready to be ploughed into the ground. The red ute crept along behind the line of flames. One side of the fire had rushed ahead, like a peak in a graph, eager to move upward and onward. Bill, from the volunteer fire service, was waiting in the lane, just in case, water tank rigged up on the back of his old Bedford. Paterson's curse still purpled up along the fence line and the cluster of ironbarks looked on from the top of the hill.

Mr Wigg had only dreamed of growing fruit commercially, any suggestion of such crazy ideas were laughed down at the pub, at bowls, and at home. 'Did you get that from one of your fancy books?' John Womersley had said, smirking into his beer. 'Wheat and sheep, mate. Wheat and sheep.' Of course that was before stone fruit took off. After that he bought all his books from mail order, rather than through the shop in town.

His son, too, had said it couldn't be done, but evidently it could. The altitude was good, summers long and dry for ripening, and the nights mostly cool: a continental climate. The Croatians had planted vines during the gold rush to make wine for themselves and sold it to prospectors on the sly. Pretty rough stuff, his father had always said, blaming it for much of the violence in the fields. These new operations were in a different league, buying up big acreage and planning for a fresh future. It wasn't often you saw life changing right before your eyes. A sign he'd hung around too long.

Mr Wigg turned back to his orchard, walked past the peaches to the trellises under the tank stand. His own grapes were looking pretty good. The sultanas were dusky brown on one side, the sugars busy forming inside. He took the secateurs from his back pocket and snipped off a draping bunch. The muscatels were turning dark, though they had a ways to go yet. He picked a couple and nibbled at them. This year he was going to try to dry some grapes, the last of the stone fruit, too. It had been his wife's suggestion, a request repeated each summer. He'd had a bit of a go, the year she died, drying apricots in the sun under muslin, but it was all very slow. He hadn't got them quite dry enough and had to wage a constant battle against ants and flies. And by then she had lost her appetite, even for apricots.

The sun was warm on his back. Mr Wigg turned off the drippers and rinsed the grapes under the tap. Cicadas shrilled in the gums shading the dam. He slid off his boots at the back door, put the grapes in the fridge, and poured himself a glass of cold cordial. Even inside he could smell the smoke.

# Workshop

He'd already sketched out a design for his fruit drying machine, and bought the fan and motor. It was high time he started on the box frame.

The workshop was still good and cool. He turned on the light over the bench and waited for it to flicker on. Cleared off everything he didn't need. He measured up the timber, marking lines with his carpenter's pencil, and then fired up the bench saw, whirring to a blur at full speed. He cut the first length, flicking the scraps away, and started on the next, pushing the timber onto the blade with both hands.

He glanced at the forge in the corner, with its old bellows. His hearing must be going, or his mind, because he kept imagining its breathing and the ring of hammer on iron. He hadn't fired it up since his wife died, hadn't had the energy.

Mrs Wigg had watched him blacksmith, when they were younger, and again when he got old. In the beginning she liked to admire him working without a shirt. By the end she'd probably started to worry he'd hurt himself, or burn the workshop down. He had made her pot-plant holders, a shelf for her recipe books, and a rack for her gardening tools. Once, in secret, he had forged a rose bud on a long stem for their anniversary. He would have liked to have been able to make her finer things, worked in silver, perhaps, rather than heavy iron.

Now half-finished hooks and pokers lay about the anvil, covered in dust. There were more than a few things he needed to catch up on. As his son liked to remind him sometimes, it wasn't right to leave so much behind for someone else to clean up.

It was high time he went over and said hello to the winegrower, Traubner, for a start. The fellow had left a note in the door, while he had been in town getting his hair cut. Mr Wigg had thought it another sympathy card at first. There had been plenty of those. They kept coming in the post for months afterwards. He still had them all in a box somewhere in the sleep-out. He should have replied to them, too, but he didn't get around to it at the time and now it seemed much too late.

It had been bothering him, the thing Fiona had said. While it was true that his wife had been sad when she died, a 'broken heart' was probably taking things a bit far. Maybe she gave up earlier than she might have otherwise, but the cancer had been all through her and nothing short of a miracle would have changed the outcome.

Mr Wigg had tried to imagine, more than a few times, the conversations that must have taken place at his son's house. Children tended to tell the truth, even when they didn't mean to, which could be a blessing and a curse. He reckoned his son's wife must have been angry at his daughter, and probably feeling bad herself. It was a shame she had said it in front of the children though. It was silly, but he didn't want them getting the idea he had hurt his wife, or that they hadn't been happy together, right up until the end.

He realised now it wasn't so much the idea of losing the property that had made his wife sad – that had hit him hardest, being his family's – it was her children fighting. And Mr Wigg not being able to get on better with his own son in those days, he supposed. Or sort any of it out.

An offcut flipped around beside the spinning blade and lodged there with an irritating *tick tick tick*. Mr Wigg reached, without thinking, to flick it away but somehow misjudged it. 'Bugger.' He turned off the saw and wrapped a cloth around his finger, trying not to see what a mess he'd made of it. *Stupid old fool.* He tried to wipe up some of the blood but just seemed to make more mess as he went.

'What the hell happened?' his son said, hurrying around to open the passenger door.

'I was just cutting some wood.'

His son frowned at the towel, blood seeping through. 'Bench saw?'

Mr Wigg nodded.

'Bloody hell, Dad. You've got Parkinson's, for Christ's sake. You could sever an artery and lie there for days before anyone even found you.'

Mr Wigg rested his hand up against his shoulder to try to slow the bleeding. Sniffed away tears. They'd be on at him to move into town again for sure now. It had started after he'd had a little fall, leaving brochures from the retirement home around and mentioning this or that nice little town house for sale. They probably wouldn't even trust him to look after the children. As if he'd ever let them get hurt.

Yellow paddocks flashed by, cut straw scored with wide tyre tracks. Heat shimmered off the road. His son drove faster. 'It's just not viable, you out there on your own, Dad,' he said. 'Especially now we're so far away.'

'Man has a right to die in his own home. You'll feel exactly the same way when you're my age.'

His son blinked, cleared his throat. They passed the graveyard at the edge of town, the newer sections freshly mown. 'I can do some of those jobs for you, you know. You just need to ask.'

'You've got more than enough to do at your place.'

'I'll make time.'

Mr Wigg nodded. He knew though, what his son thought of him spending so much time producing food he didn't need, and of 'fiddling about' in his workshop.

They pulled up in front of the hospital. Magpies sat back to back along the telephone line, like black and white pegs. His son got out to open the door. 'Okay?'

Mr Wigg nodded. Took the arm offered him. There was blood on his shirt now and he felt a bit weak. *Pathetic.*

The hundred yards to the admissions desk seemed to have stretched to a mile, the hill to have steepened. He had carried his son and daughter in more than once over the years – dog bites, barbed wire cuts, ear infections and the like – and never noticed the distance.

Mr Wigg tried to think about the cool grapes in the fridge, waiting for his morning tea. His son sat him down in a plastic chair and went to speak with the nurse.

They came back with a wheelchair, which he tried to wave away. That was the beginning of the end, right there: someone pushing you about on wheels.

'Come on, lovey,' she said. 'Don't be difficult. It's quite a ways up to surgery. Just makes it easier.'

'I'll park the car and come back and wait for you,' his son said. 'You'll be fixed up in no time.'

# Birthday Ballot

Mr Wigg sat in front of the television, his bandaged left hand resting on a fat pillow. He'd taken the top joint right off the finger, and there was no sewing it back on at his age – though his son had gone to the trouble of finding the missing piece by the forge and packing it in ice – so it was going to take a while to heal properly. It didn't hurt too much but getting to sleep would probably be difficult for a few nights. His fruit dryer was going to have to wait, after waiting so long already. He'd soon get behind on the picking and bottling, too.

His daughter-in-law had made him a chicken casserole so he wouldn't need to cook, which was good of her. His son had offered to heat some up but Mr Wigg hadn't been hungry then; the anaesthetic had left him feeling a bit queasy.

His son said he was going to drop in each day to feed the chooks and so on. He was carting wheat for some other farmers this week: long hours on top of his own farm work. Sitting in the queue at the silo in this heat. A whole lot of fuss just because Mr Wigg had shortened an already worn-out finger by half an inch. Being such a burden wasn't something he'd ever imagined as a young man, using muscle to fix most things.

He slid his glasses on and checked the television guide. There was a Hitchcock movie on a bit later, *North by Northwest*, which they had already seen, but he wouldn't mind watching again. It was one of his wife's favourites.

'Mr Heart-throb Grant is on tonight,' he said, looking over his glasses at his wife's chair. His wife was not there, of course. There was no one there. Mr Wigg blinked, swallowed the lump in his throat. He hated when he forgot; missing her hit him all over again, harder than ever.

He lowered the footrest on his chair and got up slowly, still a little light-headed. The television blared louder and the screen swam. Mr Wigg put his good hand down on the mantle to steady himself. *Good grief, it's just a fingertip.*

He shuffled out to the kitchen and dragged the casserole pot onto the heat. There was a good pile of split wood on the hearth his son must have brought in. Mr Wigg reached for a bowl from the cupboard and laid out a fork, spoon and serviette.

The box of wine the Traubners had left was sitting on the kitchen table. His son must have carried it in when they came back from hospital. A picture of gnarled old vines on the side under 'Traubner and Sons'. No problems in that family, evidently; just success. There was a nice note with it, too. In backwards-sloping handwriting so difficult to read, he'd thought it German at first.

He ducked into the dining room for a wine glass. It was a bit dusty even though it had been locked up in the sideboard. Mr Wigg put the glass down beside the sink to turn the tap on and then rinsed it under warm water, flicked it dry.

Opening the bottle was more difficult. He held it against his chest and turned in the corkscrew, leveraging it up with his right hand. It took a few goes, but he managed to release the cork with a pop. The wine was rich red, and made a significant *glub glub glub* as he filled the glass.

The casserole was bubbling. He dragged it off the heat again and managed to ladle some into his bowl, making sure he got lots of potatoes. Everything was three times as much effort with half the number of hands; it didn't really add up if you thought about it. Still, he managed. Seventy years later, there was some payoff from teachers tying his left arm behind his back and making him write with his right.

It took him three trips to ferry everything into the lounge room and by then the news had already started. He sat for a while to get his breath. There were more protests against the war in Vietnam and the Conscription Ballot was to be broadcast live after the news. He forked chicken and vegetables into his mouth and stared at the screen.

Conscription was necessary, he supposed; they'd had it in his day. And his generation hadn't baulked at doing their bit for the country. But this war in the jungle didn't seem like much of our business. It was a right mess and dragging on forever.

His son and daughter-in-law had been against it from the beginning – asking what Australia was doing blindly supporting America – going so far as to vote Labor in the last election. Everyone was talking about it; they had been the only two Labor votes taken up at the hall, not just that election, but *ever*. He had just nodded at all the guessing and gossiping, as if he had no idea who it could have been. His son hadn't told him, and he didn't need to ask; he just knew.

Some clowns even reckoned there was a communist threat in the community, went door-to-door stirring everyone up. Mr Wigg had given them some fruit and eggs at the door but turned them away. They had no business fear-mongering as far as he was concerned, like a mean preacher taking advantage of an old bloke's funeral in winter to try to scare folk back to the church.

He put his plate down to sip at the wine. Tornadoes had killed more than fifty people in America and some shiny-faced bloke called Idi Amin Dada had declared himself president of Uganda.

The chicken – one of his, his son's wife had said – was good and tender, and the casserole tasty. It could have done with more salt but he could tell she'd put some in, for his sake. The wine was good with it, smooth. And it took the edge off the throbbing in his finger.

The weather forecast was for high temperatures and strong winds later in the week. He was going to have to figure out a way to get some of his fruit off. He squashed his last potato flat with his fork and used it to mop up the meaty juice, chewing slowly. He dabbed his serviette at the gravy he'd spilt on his shirt but gave up, it would need a good soak.

He leaned down to put his plate on the floor. The Death Lottery, as objectors called it, had begun. The wooden marbles rattled round and round and they let them out one by one, announcing the numbers. The lottery machine was all wrong for the job; to win was to lose.

His son was too old now, and his daughter's husband. Their numbers hadn't come up while they were in the running, which was something to be thankful for. Someone's son would be going though, with every ball that dropped. What did blokes these days know at twenty? Not enough. And too much when they came back.

# Corvus and Dust

**M**r Wigg picked the last of the yellow-fleshed peaches one-handed. He'd waited until his son had been and gone, to avoid any fuss. There were still more on the top of the tree but he didn't want to get out the ladder, or climb with his bandaged hand; the birds could have the rest this year.

The trees were restless, unsettled by the hot wind shifting their leaves. Nobody liked a westerly. He'd given them all a good soak earlier to try to counter the drying effect but it was already an oven of a day. The figs were the chirpiest, their fruit just beginning to ripen and all that expectation still within them. They were probably thinking he'd net them today but it would have to wait till he had two hands and his land legs.

Yesterday his son had taken the last of the big machinery over to the new place, the header creeping down the road ahead of a cloud of dust, like some sort of modern day dinosaur. Mr Wigg had been supposed to drive along in front, with the 'wide load' sign, but his finger had ruled him out, injured.

The cattle would go on the weekend, a two-day walk via the stock routes. His son would be on the motorbike and his wife would help out with the ute, with the children *hup hupping* along behind.

A crow cawed from the high branches, as if calling for the fruit to ripen. The figs hissed back 'Corvus! Corvus!' trying to remind it what happened to the crow Apollo sent to fetch water from a stream. Distracted by the delicious fruit of the fig, the crow of more ancient times was late returning and tried to blame a snake. An angry Apollo flung the crow, snake and water goblet into the sky, where they remain as constellations. Being turned into a constellation didn't necessarily seem like much of a punishment to his mind, but the crow took off. It settled on a branch of the old blue gum by the dam, still calling into the heat.

The fig trees braced themselves for comment from the others but none came. The horror of birds picking holes in their fruit and defecating all over their branches was one they all shared.

'I'll give the nets a go tomorrow,' Mr Wigg said. The figs calmed and sighed, adjusting their leaves. His wife had gone to extraordinary lengths to keep the figs safe: netting, plastic bags, ice-cream buckets, a circle of scarecrows with enormous wild eyes, and, sometimes, running outside waving her arms, with her pink soapy dishwashing gloves still on, having spotted them feasting while she washed up the breakfast dishes. The year their daughter was born, she even fired his shotgun at a particularly persistent murder of crows. She managed not to hit a thing, but it sure gave him a fright down in the workshop. He'd kept the shells hidden in a separate spot after that.

Some years the fruit bats came, too, and he quite enjoyed seeing them against the dark sunsets that seemed to accompany them. They loved nothing better than eating figs, however, and sent Mrs Wigg into a war-like state. She would get out there at the first squeak of a bat and net all of the trees, and pick every day to make sure they got their share.

He carried the bucket inside and put it on the kitchen bench. The wind was picking up dust in the paddocks behind the house in brown whirls. The Traubners probably should have waited awhile before burning off. Mr Wigg had already shut all the doors and windows. He had woken with gritty eyes that morning and known what was coming. He dampened old towels and rolled them one-handed, pushing them against the verandah doors with his foot.

Outside the sky was red – dark with dust, visibility down to a few hundred yards. There had been bad dust storms the summer his daughter left home, too, as if she stirred up the very soil with her dissatisfaction. It piled up against the fences, so much so that in places the stock could just walk over them. Luckily, one brown paddock was not much different to another at that stage, and neighbours worked together to return straying animals once life returned to something more like normal.

His son had already left school to work the farm, although he could easily have gone on. The land had a way of getting into your blood, making it hard to imagine anything else. And his son had been impatient to make a start on his own life, had big plans to go into cattle. 'We have to work smarter, Dad,' he'd said. 'Not harder.'

Mr Wigg shut the blinds, closed up the kitchen and padded into the bathroom, his socks leaving damp marks on the floor. It was still difficult to get undressed with his bandaged finger. He had stopped buttoning his shirts, which was fine for summer, as long as no one turned up to see his great white belly hanging out over his shorts.

Even the cold water was tepid, heated by three days tipping a hundred and five. He fitted the plastic bag around his hand and secured it with a rubber band. It was only half a shower, really; he had to hold his plastic-wrapped hand out to make sure it didn't get wet, so he couldn't lather up or shampoo his hair. Not that there was much to wash: just a few wisps.

His daughter had always done well at school and had a real gift for art: drawing, painting, pottery – anything she put her little hands to. The house had been filled with paints and brushes; she was forever stealing his preserving jars and leaving them about with coloured water settling in the bottom. At first, he'd gone mad at her, insisted she clean up after herself. Then he came to rather like seeing the signs of her at work, mostly in blue and green. He and his wife, as well as her teachers, had assumed she would go on to teachers' college.

Everything changed when she started hanging around that Norris boy. Looking back, she had probably been in too much of a hurry to grow up, to catch up to her brother. As soon as his son started working the farm, he turned into a serious man-machine. Anything other than work was 'a waste of time' – like the occasional weekend cricket match he and Mr Wigg used to play – but the boy in him still raged over the treats and lack of responsibilities given to his sister while he 'worked his guts out'.

Meanwhile, his daughter resented that her brother had a car and was paid to work the farm – not much, mind – although she had never shown any interest in it herself. It was hard to imagine your children leaving home when they were small, let alone having minds so different from your own.

Mr Wigg turned off the tap and stepped out onto the bathmat, steadying himself on the shower door frame. He patted himself almost dry and struggled into his boxer shorts. No one would be visiting on a day like this; he could shut himself off in the cool of the lounge room and wait it out, like a fisherman in port.

Mrs Wigg had known their daughter was pregnant for several weeks and said nothing. It wasn't until after she had gone, taken off to the city, that his wife sat him down and told him. It was probably for the best, as he would have had a fair bit to say, and gone round to visit the Norrises with a fire under his hat. Still, it was a big ask for a father, not to do anything.

In the end, his daughter leaving was worst of all, though he understood why it was for the best; people round here never forgot a thing like that. But not finishing school, and a mother so young, it was hard not to be disappointed.

'She'll stay with my sister until she's had the child,' Mrs Wigg had said, in that tone signalling women's business and women's decisions already made. 'And then we'll help her get a place of her own.'

Mr Wigg had looked out at his orchard, an unfamiliar heaviness dragging on him. He had always known she would leave home eventually, he just hadn't expected it to be this soon. Or without any ceremony. 'And this secretarial school, it's nearby?'

Mrs Wigg had nodded, taken his hand. 'A block or so away; she can walk every day. Past the park. And it's not far from the water.'

Mr Wigg had felt a little better, remembering the particularities of the suburb, which was rather pleasant, really. Not the concrete uniformity he often pictured when thinking of the city. Still, tears had found their way out, when he should have been strong for his wife. And they had held each other by the window until the light left the day.

Mr Wigg sniffed and piled leftover chicken casserole onto a plate with sliced tomato, cucumber and lettuce. The wind rattled the blinds, the dust trying to force its way in.

There was a little coleslaw left, and a cold baked potato. He added a spoonful of his mayonnaise and sprinkled salt over the whole lot.

Dust already coated the verandah floor. Mr Wigg shut the kitchen door behind him and slid his clean bare feet into slippers. He shuffled down to the second fridge, leaving two dragging trails.

There was nothing like beer to get the taste of dust out of your throat. He'd learned that much driving the tractor and then the header all those years. Beer and Christmas cake, as the end of harvest approached, delivered by his daughter – with her brother's hat on to keep off the sun – for afternoon tea. It was the highlight in fields of monotony. That was life, all those little moments, you just never had the sense to realise it until they were long past.

# Autumn

Autumn

# The Fabulous Fruit Drying Machine

He still spoke to his wife every day. She didn't answer, of course, though more often than not he knew what she would have said. Today she was telling him to paint the fruit drying machine aqua.

He had managed, slowly, to finish the thing, with a bit of help from his son. His finger had healed, though the red stump was tender if he banged the end or put any pressure on it. Fiddly jobs were even more difficult than they had been before, but he could manage if he took his time. He could still grip the finger against his thumb, there was just less of it.

Mr Wigg hadn't often disagreed with his wife but he would not paint the machine aqua. It was a colour he did not miss.

He gave the dryer's timber frame a fine sand, working with the grain. The back of the front door was a little tricky but he did his best. He wiped it all down with a cloth and blew dust out of the corners. The wood was fresh and smooth under his old hands. It remained to be seen how well it worked, but it certainly looked the part.

His father had invented big practical stuff, like the portable chaff cutter they had nicknamed 'The Cyclone' for all its whirling dusty noise as it tore up hay. The Clyde engineering company had been so impressed it had produced them in three different sizes and had them on the market the following year. He and his brothers had used the original machine for another thirty years, right up until swapping to hay bales.

His son had inherited the practical genes. If a machine broke down, he'd pull out the offending part and lathe a new one himself, rather than take it to the shop. There weren't many blokes who could do that these days.

He leaned into the kitchen through the servery window to turn up the radio. England had won the Test series against New Zealand, continuing their winning streak. Only a World XI – assembled after the cancelled South African tour to England – had managed to beat them since the First Test of the 1968 Ashes series. Not bad for the team dubbed 'Dad's Army'.

With a new brush, Mr Wigg applied the first coat of varnish with shaky strokes and left it to dry. It might not be farm machinery but it would produce plenty.

The mornings were getting cooler, which was a relief after the summer they'd had. Mr Wigg put on his hat, fetched a container from the pantry and headed outside.

The Traubners were turning over the ground, their new tractor shining in the sun. Looked like they were working something into the soil, nitrogen perhaps. Years of growing wheat – his son has stopped even resting paddocks a while back, trying to keep the money coming in – would have left the soil a bit poor for their purposes.

It would probably be the last lot of figs today. The birds were taking too many, as usual, but you had to pick them ripe and he'd still have plenty to make a batch of jam. The fig trees were light-hearted, like any workers approaching the end of the job or season. They waved their limbs although there was not much breeze and chattered amongst themselves. Soon the birds would leave them alone, and they still had their leaves.

He had to make a bit of fuss over the figs; they were not the most beautiful of trees. Their fruit was actually their flower – albeit inside out – so harvest was their one chance to shine. He had tried showing the other trees a sliced fig, with their wonderful curly jam insides, but to little effect. He suspected their vision was not that good, or perhaps they chose not to see.

The figs' neighbours, the pears and apples – their fruit now set and coming on nicely as the figs' disappeared – had begun singing the inevitable 'Mr Wigg doesn't give a fig' song. The figs had learned to ignore it; it had grown rather tired after all these years.

Mr Wigg moved the ladder to get higher into the tree, his hat pushing through sandpapery leaves. A real live scarecrow; that should keep the birds away. He took his hand off the rail to wave away a fly and his foot slipped. The ladder lurched, his not inconsiderable weight all on the one side sinking it into the soft ground, and the fig tree held its breath. Mr Wigg grabbed at a branch and clung on. 'I'm fine, I'm fine,' he said.

By late afternoon the final coat of varnish was dry enough to reassemble the machine. He screwed on the timber-framed gauze sides, attached the solid top, slid in the drying trays and finally the door at the front. It was a very attractive object, even if its use may not be immediately apparent; if anything, it looked most like one of those beehive boxes you'd see gathered about in the paddocks near town. He ran an extension cord from the laundry, past the end of the hall, along the verandah to the machine.

He stopped to hear the end of the news. South Australia had won the Sheffield Shield. It was hardly a surprise given they had the Chappell brothers, and the South African import, Barry Richards. Richards had scored fifteen hundred runs in ten matches, including a triple century against Western Australia. He'd hit young Lillee all round the ground, getting him quite fired up.

Mr Wigg flicked the power on. The fan was nice and quiet, but driving a good breeze through the box. He stood to stretch his back and went to fetch the figs he had sliced earlier; they were to be his first experiment.

He lay them, not quite touching, across the four trays. One lot he had cut in half, the rest into thin slices. Some he had left the skin on, some he had peeled. The couple left over that wouldn't fit on the trays, he ate.

Now that he had finally made the machine, he couldn't help wishing he had managed it, like so many other jobs, before his wife died.

# Almond

One of Mr Wigg's orcharding books said that an almond was just a peach gone nuts. It was difficult to believe, but the peach and the almond were closely related. The almond was not, in fact, a nut at all, but a droop; an outer hull and a hard shell with the seed or nut inside. The almond trees *were* a bit nuts though, being the last to fruit and the first to flower.

Jack, the gardener up at the old farm, had given them the pair as a wedding gift, advised them where to plant them, and they had produced well from their third year. They kept to themselves, those two, a couple in their own right. He caught them singing now and then, like woodland elves, but they seemed not to talk much with the other trees, and particularly not to the peaches or nectarines. It was as if they needed to set themselves apart from those they were closest to, in order to make their own way.

Their pendulous summer shade and delicate white blossoms would probably have been enough to convince him to plant them, without their harvest. And it was an excessive harvest at that. They had picked buckets of nuts every year, in the end handing the job over to their son and daughter. Picking required ladders and climbing, and plenty of sampling of the produce, which both children adored for a time.

The real work took place after harvest. Their son and daughter took charge of the shelling, while Mrs Wigg would set to work roasting, blanching and grinding. They would put plenty away as well as eating their share of almond-flavoured sweets. His wife made her own marzipan for the Christmas cake, and an almond butter for the breakfast table. He liked to make a ground almond biscuit, with icing sugar on top. His mother had given him the recipe. From a Greek, she said. Though he couldn't remember her knowing any Greeks.

They gave plenty away, too, bagging them up and setting out a 'help yourself' stall by the mailbox. Free food always went down well, and his son and daughter would set themselves up with a notebook, recording how many cars stopped and who got out. It was their harvest, after all. Though the only one they would give away for nothing.

One year, during the picking passion, his daughter plummeted out of the male tree, like a fallen bird. Too busy cracking shells and up too high. His son, suddenly as strong as a man, had carried her inside in his arms while she screamed.

Mr Wigg had driven her to hospital, laid out across the back seat, his son holding her hand. Her arm had been broken in two places and was to be locked up in a cast for six weeks. For a time afterwards, the two of them were close and calm, peas in a pod. His son waited on her, and she appreciated it, losing Monopoly graciously for the first time in her life.

Mr Wigg moved the ladder around, keeping the sun on his back. He had filled one bucket already, and was halfway through the next. Nuts upset his stomach a bit these days, and without anyone left on the production line, he lacked the heart for processing too many for himself. His son would welcome them, though, and the children.

Saturdays weren't the same without their little faces, that's for sure. But Easter wasn't far away. It would be nice to take some almonds up to the Traubners, too. They'd probably appreciate them.

# Over the Hill

**M**r Wigg checked his figs before breakfast. The middle trays were more dehydrated than the others, a little leathery. The half figs at the top were still soft, and the flavour wonderful. Without thinking, he had packed the dryer as if it were an oven, but there was no heat to rise and the air seemed to circulate best in the middle, in front of the fan. In future he would have to rotate the trays to get a more even result. He layered the fig pieces, between baking paper, into a container and put it away in the pantry.

He ate his Weetbix out on the front verandah, watching the day start clear and cool. Today he had to take the test to see if he could keep his licence for another year: yet another of the indignities of growing old. He had been driving since he was twelve and never had an accident or a ticket in his life. Those young blokes tearing around in their hotted up Valiants and Fords were the real problem. Bill Hayland's boy

– perfectly sensible until he got that ridiculous car – rolled it on a straight road and killed himself as well as two other young fellows. They reckoned he was going over a hundred miles an hour. Only a week later, in town, another young man, Reynolds, had run into the back of a parked truck; the impact had taken his head clean off. Drunk no doubt. Four funerals and the shock of it all hadn't slowed anyone down as far as he could see.

Mr Wigg was still struggling to fasten his shirt when it was time to leave. His wife had buttoned his shirt cuffs for him even before the Parkinson's came on. His dress shirts, in particular, had such tiny buttonholes. His tremor was worse than usual this morning, which was not good timing. He'd clattered his spoon on his bowl, annoying himself nearly as much as it used to annoy his wife. The missing fingertip didn't help matters; he had to use his right hand, which was like trying to tie a knot in the mirror.

He shouldered into his jacket and pulled his sleeves down, tucked himself in. Checked he had done up his fly. It would have to do.

The ute coughed and protested, claiming a cold morning, before finally coming to life. Mr Wigg reversed out and headed up the lane. The poplars were on the turn, the green of their leaves leaching away. White trunks filled the windows as he passed, guide posts that grew larger each year, as if to counter his failing eyesight. Beyond the lane everything was bare. The big old yellow box in the middle of the paddock had been cut down, its stump burned, and the fence removed. Shallow furrows ran across the slope.

Mr Wigg stopped at the main road, looked either way and listened; there was a bit of a blind corner just before his mailbox that had always been tricky. He pulled out, giving it all the ute had and spraying up gravel. A blue Holden came flying around the corner and passed him with a whoosh, horn blaring. Mr Wigg honked his own horn and drove on. 'Bloody idiot.'

He took it easy on the way home, elbow out the open window, enjoying the wind on his face. A galah sat by the body of its mate on the side of the road, forlorn and uncomprehending. It paid to be careful driving around after harvest. All that carting of wheat back and forth from the paddocks to the silos meant a lot of spilled grain on the bitumen, attracting parrots, galahs and even cockatoos. Every year cars going too fast widowed too many birds. They must have emotions, to come back and mourn their companion like that.

Mr Wigg slowed to turn into the winemaker's driveway and pulled up in front of the shiny new shed. By the time he got out of the car, Traubner had emerged, wiping his hands on his jeans.

'Morning.'

Mr Wigg held out his hand. 'I've been meaning to drop in and thank you for the wine you left. Impressive drop.'

The winemaker took his hand and shook it. If he noticed Mr Wigg's finger stump, he was polite enough not to stare. 'You're welcome. It's good to meet you.'

Mr Wigg nodded.

'Hey, Andy,' Traubner said. 'Come out here for a sec.'

A younger version of Traubner stepped out into the sun, blinking. 'Mornin'.'

'This is Mr Wigg, James's father.'

Young Traubner shook Mr Wigg's hand. 'Pleased to meet you, sir.'

Mr Wigg smiled. 'I see you're starting to put your posts in – for the trellises?'

'Yes. Only a couple of thousand to go,' Traubner said. 'Would you like to have a look around?'

'If you have time.' He had groceries in the ute but it was in the shade for the moment.

'You right to keep going on your own?'

'No worries,' Young Traubner said. 'Nice to meet you, Mr Wigg.'

'The ute's broken down.' Traubner pulled a cloth hat from his back pocket and wiped his shiny head. 'Slowing things down a bit.'

'Mine spends most of her time parked in the shed these days – if you ever need to borrow her,' Mr Wigg said. She would be seeing out the remainder of her life on the property now; the new doctor had given him the big red light. Wasn't even going to let him drive home at first, as if he had instantly lost his faculties. His birthday present this year would be handing in his licence. He was allowed to drive up to his own mailbox and back but that was about it. Couldn't even visit his grandchildren. Marooned on his orchard island.

'I'm sure Andy will fix ours – he's so much better at that stuff than I am – but that's good to know. Thanks.'

They walked along the end of the rows, a couple of dozen timber posts already marking out their territory. The holes dug for more. Traubner took his time, pointing out this and that about the irrigation system and the variation in width between the trellises, according to the variety of grape, to allow more sun and circulation of air.

The post-hole digger stood waiting, dark brown soil still clinging to its corkscrew. A stack of treated hardwood posts towered behind it.

They passed the dam Mr Wigg and his son had dug out one winter, hiring a bulldozer for a few days. They'd had a right bust up about it, too, his son wanting to go bigger and deeper than looked right in the paddock. That night, his wife had refused to speak to either of them, slamming their plates down on the table and taking her dinner in the lounge.

Mr Wigg led the climb up to the stand of old ironbarks at the top of the hill, Traubner too polite to overtake him.

They sat on one of the granite boulders looking down over both places, while Mr Wigg puffed to get his breath back. The grass around them was burned-off brown and the hills rolled in all directions. Mr Wigg's orchard, just about starting to come into its autumn colours, nestled down on the flat, its own neat lines echoing the larger ones about it. The mountains to the west had taken on a purple tinge particular to this time of year.

The town, with its streets and roofs, had spread into the middle distance, almost to the remains of the old farm. 'Been a while since I've been up here,' Mr Wigg said.

'You're welcome to come up whenever you like,' Traubner said. 'Andy could even drive you up. When the ute's running, anyway.' He smiled.

'I might do that from time to time,' Mr Wigg said.

It was to be all cabernet sauvignon near the house, chardonnay on what had been the three hundred acres, and riesling on the slope by the road. There was another grape, Tempranillo, going in, which was Spanish not German, and better suited to the climate. 'In the meantime, we're going to use grapes from home, and around the place, to start making our own.' He pointed out where the shed would go, and described a cellar door and shop.

Mr Wigg blinked. 'My son will like that,' he said. 'They took a trip to the Barossa last year and came back raving about it. Got some nice wines, too.'

'That's where my family is from,' Traubner said. 'My grandfather started his first vineyard back in 1849.'

'You didn't want to stay around there?'

'It's like Little Germany. Too much tradition. I wanted to make a new start somewhere,' he said. 'Besides, my brother got the family vineyard, so I've got to make my own way.'

'My grandfather came out around the same time. Gold,' he said. 'Bought up all this land, almost to the edge of town.' He pointed, forgetting his stump. 'I can't really see it from here anymore, but there used to be a village where the road kinks – Council never paid us for that road either, mind. At the height of the gold rush there was a school, a shop, bakery, blacksmith, cricket pitch, and pubs and a cellar. And a big orchard, of course. Most of the buildings are still standing.'

'You grew up there?'

Mr Wigg nodded. 'It hadn't really taken off for farming then. My father added a shearing shed and tennis court, fenced it all and put in dams. My brothers and I – there were four of us – got a quarter each when my father went.'

'That's fair.'

'James, he was the eldest, got the old farm but he died young and didn't have any sons. I would really have liked to buy it back but times were tough then; we came straight out of the Depression and into the war. Francis sold his and became a teacher. Herb's place went to his wife's family when he died – he served in France – and then got sold off . . .'

Traubner rubbed his knuckles. 'What ship did your grandfather come out on?'

'Captained his own ship. He was a deep sea pilot back in Scotland. Sailed into Melbourne then travelled up through the goldfields. Ended up here. A long way from the ocean.'

'Bit of an adventurer, then?'

'I didn't inherit much of that, I'm afraid. I like the water but have never sailed. Or ever been overseas, for that matter.' And now he couldn't even leave what was left of his property. You spent most of your life working to try to build something, to make something for yourself, your children. Only to watch it all fall away.

'I dunno. I reckon living in this country, with that great big interior, it's kinda like sailing. There's so much space, you know. Opportunity.' Traubner's face had taken on a dreamy look.

'Well,' Mr Wigg said. 'I hadn't thought of it like that.'

# Quince

**M**r Wigg fondled a quince. Their golden roundness always conjured up images of old paintings: bowls of voluptuous fruit on dark timbered tables. He rubbed away the last of its woolly fuzz with his thumb and smelled the skin.

*'They dined on mince and slices of quince, which they ate with a runcible spoon.'*

The trees sang along, waving their long leaves. He and his wife had been married in autumn, as the Owl and the Pussycat must have been. They had not had quince or mince at their wedding, which was a shame. Dancing by the light of the moon would have been far more romantic than all that church formality. Still, it had been the happiest day of his life, seeing her come down the aisle towards him, her white dress lit up in the morning sun, like some sort of angel.

According to the book his wife had given him on the history of fruit, quince was a traditional offering at weddings in ancient Greece. It was the fruit Paris gave Aphrodite, and Hippomenes had apparently caught the bear-suckled huntress, Atlanta, in a footrace (and marriage) by throwing her three quinces to slow her down. Some scholars even thought the apple from the Garden of Eden was actually a quince. Thinking about all that temptation might change some people's ideas about the fruit.

If he could have his wedding over, he would have them piled high in silver bowls on every table, instead of flowers.

*'They sailed away for a year and a day.'*

The neighbouring pears, distant relations to the quince, hummed, too. Their fruit would be the next to ripen. An allegiance in the orchard was a good thing, protecting the quince from inevitable taunts about fruit that cannot be eaten unless cooked for hours and hours. Insults like 'boot leather' and 'horse fodder' had been tossed around at first.

Before the pears were of fruit-bearing age, an orchard-wide argument had raged about marmalade, of all things. The oranges insisted marmalade had always been made from citrus. The wiser quince, albeit with obvious self-interest, felt obliged to point out that, in fact, marmalade is a bastardisation of the Portuguese word, *marmelo*, meaning quince, and all marmalade was made from quinces until the Scots invented orange marmalade in 1790. Mr Wigg much preferred orange marmalade, or cumquat, but tried not to let that thought even cross his mind while about the quince trees. Mrs Wigg hated marmalade altogether, and anything with peel in it. If accidentally putting anything containing peel to her mouth, she would screw up her face as if she had licked a cut lemon.

He hooked the bucket on the side of the ladder, put the first quince in, and reached for the top fruit. They were ready to fall, just needing a nudge to drop into his hand.

A cloud of dust at the top of the lane signalled a visitor coming down too fast. His wife had put up 'go slow' signs years ago – in neat white block letters – to little effect. His son's ute pulled up out the front. Mr Wigg frowned; it wasn't Wednesday. Or was it?

Mr Wigg stretched for the last couple of quince from the tree's crown, giving up when the ladder began to teeter. He heard his son come tramping across the furrows, more dust flying up from his boots.

'What happened, Dad?'

'Eh?'

'The doctor rang; he said you've lost your licence.'

Mr Wigg looked down from the ladder. So much for doctor–patient confidentiality.

'Was it your eyesight? Did you remember to take your glasses?'

'I think it was the whole package,' he said. 'Being old.' He had tried to hide his finger, and his tremor, but the new doctor from the city had sharp eyes and firm ideas about doing everything by the book. 'Mind you, Harry bloody Needham still has his licence, and he's ten years older than me and blind in one eye!'

His son broke up a clod. 'Things can't go on like this.'

Mr Wigg unhooked the bucket and handed it down. 'Well, apparently they can; there are plenty of other people in my situation.'

'I guess I could bring your groceries out,' his son said, taking the bucket with both hands.

Mr Wigg climbed down. 'There's a service. The supermarket boy will bring it out for me; I just have to ring up with what I want each week, they said.'

His son nodded. 'What about bowls?'

'I haven't been going for a while now.'

'Things would be a lot easier if you moved into town, Dad.'

They watched a hawk hovering above the orchard. There was not a waft of cloud to interrupt the blue. The hawk dived, snared a mouse, and settled on a fence post to enjoy it.

'Will you at least ask us if you need anything, or want to go anywhere?'

'Where would I go?' Mr Wigg shrugged. He took the bucket from his son. 'Come inside, I want to show you something.'

His son peered inside the drying machine, chewing on a piece of dried fig. 'Huh.' He opened and shut the door, slid the trays in and out. Compared the drawings to the finished machine. 'This is great.' He picked up a ring of dried apple, examined it and popped it in his mouth.

'I'll put lemon on next time, to stop it going brown,' Mr Wigg said.

'You could sell these.' His son rubbed at his chin, spun the machine's fan with his finger. He had grown a beard, as was the fashion, and left his hair longer. Somehow it made him look younger. 'You should patent the design, Dad. Take it to the Field Days and see if you can get it picked up.'

Mr Wigg smiled.

His son selected another apple ring. 'I'll find out how to do it,' he said. 'I reckon there'd be a big demand for them.'

'You think so?'

# Cupcakes

'Poppy, can we make cupcakes this time?' Fiona said, before Mr Wigg could even close the screen door behind them.

'I thought we were going to make marble cake,' Lachlan said.

'Right,' said Mr Wigg. 'So let's make marble cake *and* some cupcakes. With orange icing.'

'Really?'

'Cool!' said Lachlan.

Mr Wigg set Lachlan up at the bench with the beaters, creaming butter and sugar, and sent Fiona off to the pantry for cocoa, cochineal and an orange. It was good to have some little helpers. Mrs Wigg had found them altogether too messy to cook with – mopping the floor furiously after every visit – but he didn't mind. They wouldn't learn to clean up after themselves by not cooking.

Fiona returned carrying the ingredients before her with great seriousness. 'Is it the red colouring that's made from squashed beetles?'

Lachlan screwed up his nose. 'Yuk.'

'That's right: the cochineal. It's a very special insect,' Mr Wigg said. 'Did you know it only lives in cactus?' He held the little bottle up to the light. 'Captain Arthur Phillip brought the prickly pear to Australia to try to start a cochineal industry. All the beetles died but prickly pear grew like nobody's business.'

'Dad told us about that,' Lachlan said. 'And then they had to introduce a moth to get rid of the prickly pear.'

'There's a lesson there. Introducing plants and animals from somewhere else can have unintended consequences.'

Lachlan peered into the bowl. 'Do I add the eggs now?'

'That's right. One at a time.'

'Can I make the icing?' Fiona said.

'We're not quite ready for that yet. Why don't you grease the pan, and set out the patty papers.'

'Okay.' Fiona put on her serious 'I'm going to work' face. The very image of her father.

'Are you having fun at the new farm?'

Fiona shrugged.

'It's okay,' Lachlan said.

Mr Wigg inspected the cake mixture. 'Excellent. Now just sieve in the flour and mix it through.' He pulled two glass bowls out from the cupboard. 'That will do. Now pop a third of the mixture into this bowl. We're going to add cocoa to this one.'

Lachlan poured until Mr Wigg held up his hand.

'Okay, now we just want to add a bit more flour to your remaining mixture, then pour another third into this bowl,' he said. 'We're going to add Beetle Juice to this one.'

'Poppy!' they said.

'It's only a few drops,' he said.

'Does strawberry milk have the cottoneel beetle in it?'

Lachlan groaned. 'It's got *strawberries* in it, stupid.'

'I knew *that*,' said Fiona.

Lachlan poured most of the chocolate mixture into one corner, and Fiona managed the pink. Mr Wigg followed up with the vanilla. 'Now I like to give it a swirl with the spatula, to mix the colours up a bit more.'

The children watched with their mouths open.

Lachlan held the oven door open and Mr Wigg slid in the tin. 'Fiona, you set the timer now. Fifty minutes.'

'Okay,' she said.

'The rest of the mixture is for the cupcakes. You guys can do those on your own.'

'Can we use all three colours?' Lachlan said.

Mr Wigg nodded and sat down at the kitchen table.

'I want to make one that's all chocolate,' Fiona said.

Lachlan giggled. 'And I'll make one that's all pink.' He helped his sister put the tray in the oven. 'Quickly,' he said.

'What are we doing now?' Fiona said, the minute the oven door was closed.

Mr Wigg rubbed his face. 'Well, it won't be long till the cupcakes are cooked. Twelve or fifteen minutes. Why don't we clean up and then we can do the icing?'

'Okay,' she said.

Mr Wigg pushed himself to his feet. 'Can you grab an extra tea towel, please, Fiona?'

Lachlan was doing a pretty good job of wiping down the benches, and clearing all the dishes to the left of the sink the way Mr Wigg liked. Mr Wigg ran the hot water, letting it warm his hands before he added the detergent.

Fiona returned with a striped aqua tea towel – three different shades – and dragged the stool over to the bench. 'Do you have a story today, Poppy?'

Mr Wigg lifted her up onto the stool. 'Hmmm,' he said.

'Whatever happened to that peach tree?' Lachlan said.

'Do you mean the first ever peach tree in the kingdom of the Orchard Queen?'

'Yes!'

'It had sprung up, quite by accident, you know: a chance seedling from another tree. Or perhaps a bird carried the seed from far away and dropped it by the bank of a stream in the middle of a forest. It was a wonderful spot to grow up.

'So when the queen's gardener was walking in the forest and saw the tree's beautiful pink blossom, he decided the Orchard Queen *must* have this tree in her collection.' Mr Wigg placed another dripping bowl on the dish rack. 'But . . . he had to wait until the end of autumn, when the peach tree was dormant, to move it.'

'What's dormet?' Fiona said.

'Asleep. After the flowers have turned into fruit and the fruit gets ripe and all of the tree's leaves fall off, it has a sleep for the winter. That's the best time to move a fruit tree,' Mr Wigg said. 'And the queen's gardener knew this, so he had to wait. But he took back some blossom for the queen's table.

'The queen was impatient, asking that the tree be brought to her at once, but the queen's gardener – he was a very wise old man – convinced her that the tree would die if moved while blooming.

'When summer was on its way, the gardener visited the peach tree, giving it a light prune to help it channel all its energy into making fruit. The tree was a bit shocked but had heard stories about the queen's magical gardener and trusted that this must be one of his tricks.

'Towards the end of summer, the gardener came back again. Can you guess why?'

'To pick the peaches,' Lachlan said.

'Exactly. The queen's gardener brought a wicker basket lined with purple felt. The peaches were enormous and perfectly ripe. He plucked one off and smelled the skin. Then he took his first bite. Peach juice dribbled down his chin and onto his shirt and he knew the little tree was very special. It was the best fruit he had ever tasted.

'The gardener picked the six biggest, ripest peaches and carried them carefully back for the queen.

'The Queen of Orchards had a servant slice her up a peach. And then another, and another. The gardener stood back from the table, waiting. The queen smiled – and it was not often that she smiled – "Bring me *more*," she said.

"'The tree is only young, your Majesty," the gardener said. "There are not many fruit."

"'I want them *all*," she said. "No one must know of this *divine* fruit until the tree is in *my* orchard."

'The queen's gardener hurried back out to the forest with his basket. It was still warm, but the sun was setting, and the shadows growing long. He had trouble finding his way. A wolf howled in the next valley. By the time he returned to the peach tree, it was almost dark. He reached for a fruit but found that they were all gone. Every one.

'The queen's gardener wished he had told the queen there were no more, because now she was going to be very angry. Just then, he heard giggling. He felt his way along a path to a small clearing.

'There in the long grass, was a young woman eating peaches with a gypsy boy. "Stop!" he said. "Those are the queen's fruit!"

'The boy turned, his face barely visible in the dusk light, but his teeth shone white. "These peaches belong to no one. They grow wild."

'The young woman kept her face turned away but the gardener knew her, for he had seen her every day for sixteen years. "Daughter! Come away from that poacher and bring me those last peaches. The queen herself has sent for them."

'His daughter took the boy's hand. "You may bend low for the queen, but I will not."

'"Then do as your father bids you."

'His daughter stood. She held a peach in each hand. The gypsy boy gathered up their things. And they turned and ran away into the forest.

'The Orchard Queen was very angry. She asked again that the peach tree be brought to the safety of her orchard. Again, the queen's gardener explained that the transplantation could not take place until late autumn. The queen banged her goblet on the table. "I am sick of those gypsies thieving from my lands," she said. "I should not have to wall everything up in an orchard."

'The gardener looked at his feet. He could not tell the queen his own daughter had run off to live with the gypsies. He blamed himself; everyone had said it was foolish, trying to raise a girl alone after her mother died.

'And so the queen ordered her soldiers to drive the gypsies, and all their bright caravans, from her lands.'

Fiona frowned.

Mr Wigg let out the sink water and began putting dishes away. 'The gardener was very sad. He tended to the pruning in the queen's orchard, and sought news of his daughter from every traveller. He walked in the forest every day listening for her laugh. One morning in late autumn, he took a shovel, sackcloth and basket, all strapped to his back, into the forest to dig up the little peach tree.

'Hanging in the peach's bare branches was . . . his daughter's locket.'

Fiona clapped her little hands together, dropping the tea towel on the floor. 'She's all right?'

'Yes,' Mr Wigg said. 'And the peach tree lived happily ever after in the queen's orchard with the other fruit trees. And the gypsies grew peach trees wherever they went.'

Fiona hugged his legs. 'Did you make up that story?'

'No,' he said. 'The Peach King told me.'

'There's a king of peaches?' Fiona said.

Lachlan laughed.

'There most certainly is,' Mr Wigg said. 'But now it's time to liberate these cupcakes.'

# Pomegranate

Mr Wigg had often thought that the pomegranate should fruit in summer, as its shiny red globes most resembled, to his mind, Christmas baubles. They were festive in a fruit bowl or on a table, and all that red juice made for a wonderful sauce for the turkey. Today not even their colour could cheer him.

It had been his wife's request to grow a pair, one of the more decorative of the fruit trees. Their orange, trumpet-like flowers came on in late summer, just when things were feeling too hot, dry and bleak. He'd grown them on 'her' side of the orchard, so that she could see them from parts of her garden. She had grown a dwarf ornamental to mirror them. Its flowers were more grand, and oversized for the tree. Its fruit set more like rosehips, as if never quite coming to fruition.

Mr Wigg broke open the ripest of the fruit, crimson juice spraying up his wrist and onto his shirt. The seeds nestled in neat rows like damp jewels. He separated a cluster from the white pulp and sucked the red flesh, spitting the seeds out onto the ground. Named from the Latin for 'seeded apple', it was true pomegranates were nearly all seeds, but the flavour was worth the trouble. He used to make a cordial out of them, or a syrup for cooking. And Mrs Wigg had liked to sprinkle them over her orange salad.

According to Greek myth, Hades tricked Persephone into eating six pomegranate seeds while in the Underworld, condemning her to six months down there each year. Mr Wigg licked his lips; he understood perfectly well why she had been unable to resist the temptation.

If only he could spend six months of the year with his wife – not that he thought she would have been sent to any Underworld – by eating such a delicacy. But then, who would look after his orchard during winter and autumn?

The other trees were somewhat reverential towards the pomegranate; it had never been the object of ridicule or scorn. Perhaps it was its beauty, its arching branches and pleasing flower, or its lineage; he did not know. Like so many fruit, they had originated in Persia, and opening them up each season still had him imagining carpets, camels and copper pots. Fruit was a way to travel the world without leaving home.

They were the quiet trees of the orchard, always speaking in low tones. When his son and daughter were small, he had read them the *Tales of the Arabian Nights* out by the pomegranates, hoping to build a bit of atmosphere. His daughter quite often went to sleep, being a little young for such big adventures, but once, when she woke, she said the pomegranates had been telling her their own stories, in which trees played a much more prominent role.

Mr Wigg picked an armful of fruit for the wooden bowl in the dining room. He would have grown them for their aesthetic value even if they were only half as delicious. Perhaps this year he would make syrup again.

His daughter had liked to help him separate all the seeds from the pithy flesh – popping as many into her mouth as the sieve – and then using a heavy spoon to juice them. All you needed was the juice and sugar for the most exquisite colour and flavour. Mr Wigg and his daughter would hang around in the kitchen while the syrup reduced, playing snap. Though he had to let her win, or see her mood change.

She would draw decorative labels for the bottles, once they cooled, and stack them away in the pantry. Months later, they made a fancy addition to a Christmas hamper, or did as an emergency gift if someone unexpected turned up.

Her labels got more and more sophisticated as she grew older, with fancy lettering. Some years she would label all of the preserves. He supposed it should have been no surprise that his daughter should excel at drawing fruit.

# Poire

After breakfast, Mr Wigg had another go at sketching the Peach King; it was easier without the leaves, freeing him up to focus on its structure, the way the branches fanned outwards and upwards. It was becoming something else, this tree; after all, it didn't have to produce fruit or defend itself against disease. The branch tips began to entwine their fingers as if let go for a season or two.

He stood up to turn the page on the calendar – it was nearly a week into the new month already – and stuck his latest drawing over the picture of a new header. Farm machinery never did make for very interesting photos but you couldn't expect much for free. It was either that or a bowl of fruit on the grocer's complimentary calendar. They were always rolled up too tight, as well, and no amount of flattening under books could set them right.

He made a mark on the calendar out of habit: their anniversary. It was not as if the date ceased to exist, or that either of them had chosen to end the marriage, but it was no longer a happy day.

*'Pears for their heirs. Pears for their heirs.'*

While loyal, and their accents beautiful, Mr Wigg's pear trees were not particularly imaginative. Mr Wigg filled a bucket with still-firm fruit from the Williams' Bon Chrétien. French pears had been all the go in the 1700s and Bon Chrétien was named to appeal to the market. When it reached America, however, the importer, Mr Bartlett, evidently a small man, promptly named it after himself. Mr Wigg liked to insist upon the original.

His mother's side had been French. It probably showed in her cooking, though he'd never heard her speak more than the occasional phrase. *Beurre blanc* and so on. Bon Chrétien whispered its drooping companion, the Belgian Beurré Bosc, a few words of reassurance; its elongated russet fruit were a ways off ripe. *'Pears for their heirs. Pears for their heirs.'*

That's what people used to say; that wise gardeners planted pears for their heirs. His orchard, however, all that was left of the Wigg legacy, would not now go to his descendants, but likely get sold off like everything else. It would help his son and his family, he supposed, and that was something.

Mr Wigg pushed his way deeper into the tree. It had supposedly been the Romans who introduced pears to France.

The frescos of Pompeii featured pears very much like those he was picking today. The Romans didn't eat them raw, but cooked them up with honey. Perhaps they had picked them too green.

It was the Greeks who had written about pears first though; in Homer's *The Odyssey*, the pear was one of the 'gifts of the gods' growing in the garden of Alcinous, the King of the Phaeacians:

*Outside the courtyard, fronting the high gates,*
*a magnificent orchard stretches four acres deep*
*with a strong fence running round it side-to-side.*
*Here, luxuriant trees are always in their prime,*
*pomegranates and pears, and apples glowing red,*
*succulent figs and olives, swelling sleek and dark.*
*And the yield of these trees will never flag or die,*
*neither in winter nor in summer, a harvest all year round*
*for the West Wind always breathing through will bring*
*some fruits to the bud and others warm to ripeness –*
*pear mellowing ripe on pear, apple on apple,*
*cluster of grapes on cluster, fig crowding fig.*

'Pear upon pear,' the trees echoed. Mr Wigg had memorised that piece for a school recital. The teacher had looked a bit surprised; the other boys all chose bloody battle scenes or the bit with the bare-breasted sirens.

A west wind was never a good thing on this side of the world but walking in such an ancient orchard was how Mr Wigg imagined heaven. He couldn't decide, though, on the best season in which to enjoy it. Spring for its blossoms, autumn for its colour, but to not sample the fruit would be a shame. Summer perhaps, and a picnic in the shade with his wife. Glasses of champagne tilted towards each other, and a platter of sliced fruit between them.

His bucket now full, Mr Wigg carried it inside. It was vanity, he supposed, wanting his orchard to carry on. One of his descendants to value it, if not him. His daughter had been interested, in her way, painting some nice still lifes. There was one of him in the orchard, too, picking oranges, still hanging in the dining room. He'd been a bit younger and thinner then – more bulk up top, less down below – but it was quite a good likeness.

Mr Wigg had been picking oranges the day everything began to come to a head, although he hadn't realised it at the time. His son had buzzed across the paddocks on the old motorbike, a Honda he'd had then, puffing smoke out the back. A cloud of dust behind him as usual.

'Do you know what time it is?' His son had said, from beneath the tree. Flies covered the shoulders of his shirt.

Mr Wigg had looked at his watch. 'Ah.' And climbed down from the ladder.

'I've been on the tractor since four in the bloody morning,' he'd said, red in the face. 'You were supposed to relieve me at ten.'

'I lost track of time. I'll go now, it'll be fine.'

'It's *not* fine, Marg had to drive herself to hospital for her ultrasound and we're behind on the spraying.'

Mr Wigg had leaned on the ladder. It was the child who would be Lachlan on the way, after a couple of false starts, and no doubt his son was worried. 'Sorry.' He had meant to be there early, had packed his esky right after breakfast.

'I can't take it,' his son had said. 'I'm killing myself trying to make us all a living and you're busy making jam and milking the cows just to feed the dogs.'

Mr Wigg had blinked. He still had milking cows and working dogs in those days. Once the kids grew up, they didn't use as much milk – though Mrs Wigg still liked to make ice-cream now and then – but the cows still needed milking and he didn't see the harm in giving the leftovers to the dogs.

'It's such a waste of time, Dad. You're too busy producing food to generate any income. It's all the wrong way round.'

'I'm always happy to do my share of the farming.'

His son had pulled an orange from the tree and pushed his thumb through the rind. 'You're not doing your share. You leave most of the real work to me. And yet you insist on doing everything your way. The stupid, slow, old way.'

'Now just hang on a minute,' Mr Wigg had said, hot under his hat. 'You wanted to try the cattle feedlot idea, I agreed with that.'

'After I nagged you for more than a year.'

'If you need me to pay you more –'

'I don't want you paying me at all, Dad. I want to make my own way!'

# Perry

Mr Wigg halved another batch of pears for drying. He was really getting the hang of the dehydrating machine, setting up a timer to remind him when to rotate the trays and another on the power point that turned off automatically when they were done.

He was building up quite a store of dried fruit. This year, he reckoned he could make his Christmas cake and pudding all from his own orchard. Except the flour and sugar.

It was another clear day but Mr Wigg had seen all the ants out this morning, stocking up and fortifying their nests. There was proper rain coming. His son would be hoping to start the ploughing when it did. And the Traubners were out early in straw hats, stringing the wires on the trellis, as if they, too, knew the change was coming. They were on the slope above the house, and Mr Wigg almost thought he could hear the winch tightening the wires.

He carried in the finished trays of shrivelled golden pears, yesterday's batch, to pack away into jars. They were firm but still a little moist, and full of wonderful flavour. Shakespeare, for all his fine ability with the word, clearly had not appreciated pears, for they did not get one positive mention in all of his works. In *The Merry Wives of Windsor*, Falstaff imagines the court whipping him with their fine wits until he was 'as crest-fallen as a dried pear'. In *Romeo and Juliet*, Mercutio makes rather unsavoury remarks about poor old Romeo, using the 'open arsed' medlar and long, tapering Poperin pear as euphemisms. Given the Poperin pear was now thought to be extinct, it seemed rather a shame that it might be remembered in such a vulgar context.

His wife had always maintained that such things should not be the butt of jokes, or discussed outside the bedroom. It wasn't that she lacked a sense of humour, or was in any way prudish, but she had firm ideas about what was proper.

He spread the new pear halves out evenly over the trays, and packed them into the machine. They lay beside one another in golden expectancy, awaiting their next stage in life. It was hard not to notice their lovely feminine shape; surely deserving of more poetic representation.

There were two more buckets of pears on the sink but Mr Wigg had something else in mind for them.

Mr Wigg peeled the pears first, and set the skins to one side. This lot had been resting in the pantry for a couple of days and had softened nicely. He chopped them into rough chunks and, with the back of the knife, scraped them into the juicer he had propped on a new bucket in the sink.

He turned the handle slowly to extract the juice, the blade forcing the fruit over the sieve. The pulp would go to the chooks, sending them into a pecking frenzy. If he threw it to them every day, they'd soon turn up their noses; this way it was recognised as a once-a-year treat.

When the process was complete, he had three-quarters of a bucket of juice and a messy kitchen. Mr Wigg added the peels to the bucket, put the lid on, and carried it into the dark cool of the pantry. The yeasts in the peel would start the fermentation process. His weren't proper Perry pears, which were descended from 'wildings' – self-made hybrids of the cultivated and wild pear, much higher in yeasts and tannins – but it still seemed to work.

He wiped down the benches and washed up the juicer, humming to himself. The Year Everything Went Wrong, his pear cider had exploded. It had been a hot day: not yet summer, but signalling its approach. He had heard the first bang, like a gunshot, from the orchard and come running. It had been followed by another and another and another, in even succession. He had torn inside with one boot still on to find his wife safe and sound, standing with her arms crossed, outside the pantry door. There were only three bottles left and he'd hopped across the wet floor and climbed up to try to save them. Another exploded as he reached for it, its lid leaving a dint in the ceiling. Cider rained down over him, dripped off the shelves. He had rushed the last two bottles into the fridge and breathed. Somehow, the fermentation process had kept going in the bottle, rather than exhausting its yeasts. Too much sugar. He had got something wrong, with so much on his mind.

His wife had fetched the mop and bucket, some towels and then disappeared. He had spent the better part of the afternoon cleaning up; the cider dried sticky and every surface, right down to the last jar, had to be wiped twice.

It had never happened before or since. When he drank a glass of that troublesome perry, later that afternoon, it had been twice as strong as usual. His wife had found him asleep on the lounge room floor.

'Dinner.'

'Huh?' Mr Wigg rubbed his eyes.

'Dinner is on the table,' Mrs Wigg said.

'Coming.'

She put her hand in his and helped him up. 'Nice sleep?'

'Must be tired,' he said, rubbing his face. He sat down at the table. Put his serviette on his lap. 'Thank you.' She had made roast pork and apple sauce, with little beets and beans on the side.

She smiled.

He picked up his knife and fork. 'I've been thinking,' he said. 'That maybe I should retire, and hand over the farm. Like he wants.'

She cut a sliver of pork and spread apple sauce over it. 'Is that what you want?'

Mr Wigg nodded. 'I'm getting old.'

'We both are.' She chewed her mouthful. 'We'd still be here to help out,' she said. 'If they need it.'

'That's right,' he said. 'We'll be right next door.'

'Then I think we should go ahead.'

Mr Wigg cut his beans in half. 'He suggested we keep the house paddocks, maybe lease them out for a bit of income.'

'The O'Briens will probably be interested.' She pushed her food around the plate with her fork. 'We should try to give Deb something, too. To help her buy a house.'

'That's a good idea.' Mr Wigg crunched on crackling. 'We'll do that.'

# Pruning

**M**r Wigg began with the yellow peach trees, cutting back any dead or damaged branches. He shortened the wood that had borne fruit down to one or two buds. The buds would produce spring's new growth and blossom, producing fruit the following year; with the peaches and nectarines, pruning was always part of a two-year plan.

He gathered up the offcuts, piled them into the wheelbarrow and moved on to the nectarines. Storms the year before had damaged one of the crowns, so he'd cut out both their centres completely. It had looked a bit drastic at first, and they had produced less fruit, but what there was had come on larger and more sweet.

It wasn't as if he needed much anyway, with just himself to feed. He didn't tend to cook with them, just ate them fresh. The nectarines' new growth had taken on a weeping look and he pruned lightly to encourage that further. They were really just a peach with smooth skin, or that's how they had started out, anyway: a peach with a recessive gene. His mother had said that the nectarines up at the old farm used to produce the occasional furry fruit, like some sort of throwback.

Inevitably, the peaches tossed about terms like 'mutant', and 'slip skin', which he tried to discourage; nectarines tended to bruise easily.

The sun was overhead now, although it had little warmth in it. A breeze from the south ran up between the rows of trees, getting right behind his ears. The Traubners were still stringing trellises, probably getting sick of the job.

The citrus blossom was out – orange and lemon – all waxy and white. He had made orange blossom water one year, and used it in desserts for the winter. A lot of trouble though, and he preferred to see them on the tree. His son had brought back honey made with the flowers of an orange orchard once, from somewhere down in Victoria. Mr Wigg had licked it from the teaspoon, unable to believe how much it tasted of oranges. He had daydreamed about producing peach honey, even nectarine or apricot, but never got around to it.

His son had kept bees for a while, as a boy, had a few hives under the trees by the dam. Yellow box made good honey, and ironbark. Less discriminating folk set up in a paddock of Paterson's curse – lord knows there was plenty of it, with no known use but to itch your legs – but it made for an inferior honey: smoky and bland.

Mr Wigg emptied the wheelbarrow on the rubbish pile and moved on to the apricot trees. Their size required the ladder and a bit more patience. He sawed off a few bits of dead wood and then set about cutting out the crowded laterals, wiping his secateurs with metho-soaked cloth after each cut. He shortened the vigorous shoots by about two-thirds, to maintain shape and encourage more shooting spurs. The apricots bore their fruit on one-year-old wood as well as the short-lived spurs on older wood; pruning was a two-pronged attack.

The trees fell quiet while being pruned; and those yet to go under the blade looked on soberly. Mr Wigg expected it caused them some pain, but they had never complained. It seemed they understood the necessity of it, and trusted him to do it properly. Without pruning, without him, they were more prone to disease, and the quality of their fruit would diminish.

Mr Wigg gathered up the discarded pieces and dropped armfuls into the barrow. Above him, the apricot sighed with relief. Hummed a quiet song as if to balm and salve itself.

Handing over the farm had seemed like a big deal while he had been chewing it over, as if admitting yet another defeat. As soon as the decision was made, though, he had felt lighter, as if all his father's expectations had been removed, and all the work he didn't enjoy cut away.

He and his wife had tried not to load all those pressures on to their own son, to teach him about enjoying life, too. Not that they had been particularly successful on that front.

The way he saw it, raising children was a lot like pruning; you needed to ensure a stable structure and then encourage fruitful growth, rather than allowing them to waste their energy. Sometimes, though, what they leaned towards was the very opposite of what you meant to impart.

# Persimmons

The persimmon trees lit up the centre of the orchard, their leaves bright smudges of copper and crimson, like an oil painting. Mr Wigg walked towards them, trying to bring them into some sort of focus. He dropped the nets on the ground and checked over the fruit on each tree, fully formed and beginning to ripen. The pale orange globes were only visible once you got close, outshone, for the moment, by the brighter leaves. The trees wore their name, *Diospyros kaki* or 'food of the gods', with pride, their weeping limbs the only sign of any burden of expectation.

He went back for the ladder, carrying it under his arm, whistling. Every season had its work, and its joys. He uprighted the ladder beside one of the trees. It was a shame to ruin the look of them but if he wanted any fruit for himself they had to be netted.

He climbed the ladder and threw one net out over the lower branches, a bit like a fisherman. It was the opposite of fishing really, the net designed to keep things out rather than drag them in. He manoeuvred the ladder in among the branches to spread the net's reach. The birds were welcome to the fruit above the net line, which he could no longer reach anyway.

The persimmons' fruit clustered on the outer edges of the tree, borne of last year's growth, and anxious to secure the best view out to the world. The persimmons often squabbled with the other trees, quick to boast of their superior autumn shades and their ancestry as providers to the gods.

The more pragmatic peaches tried reminding the persimmons of the peach's even longer history gracing the tables of emperors and kings – who, unlike gods, actually existed – for their quality of ensuring long life.

The persimmons, quick to retort, pointed out the contradiction of denying the existence of the gods while believing in their own mythical powers, and drew attention to their relative positions in the orchard – the persimmons' centre stage signalling superiority to the peaches' outer edge.

To which, the peaches, finally losing their temper, would snort and mutter something unkind about the character of trees whose fruit ripens in winter.

Mr Wigg smiled and shook his head, hoisting the ladder onto his shoulder and carrying it back to the workshop.

The smell of fresh bread – from today's grocery delivery – had his stomach grumbling. He cut a thin slice to nibble on while he made his sandwiches. The cook, Mrs Kurzer, had baked loaves every day up at the old farm. She had been the tallest woman he had ever seen, which was just as well, as the door to the old brick oven was chest height on a man. His father used to lend her the horse and sulky to go home every couple of weeks. She would return after dark, perhaps to ensure she missed all the chores of the evening meal. One night, though, she thought she saw a ghost carrying his head under his arm, and after that she always returned in daylight.

Mr Wigg cut up the last of the roast beef, and added cheese, tomato and lettuce. He spread peach chutney over the top slice of bread. His parents had got rid of the bread oven when they did the place up, which he'd thought a shame even as a boy, despite his father's scary stories about witches cooking children inside it. The bakery in town started delivering twice a week, then, and the neighbours from further up the road would come by in the morning to collect their loaves and catch up on gossip.

The bakery had still delivered bread to everyone's mail-boxes in a brown paper bag until after the children left home. Young Mr Parker and his wife had taken over by then. People said you could tell when they had had a fight; the bread was burned quite black on one side.

Mr Wigg sat at the table to eat his sandwich. His wife had taught their daughter-in-law to bake bread. And to stew and bottle fruit. As a new wife, and new to farm life, she had been keen to learn.

Mrs Wigg probably overdid it a bit, though, popping up nearly every day. It was always to help with this or that and she meant well, but of course young people want to do things their own way.

He knew there'd be trouble when she offered to help paint the new nursery. She had spent quite a few years worrying there would be no grandchildren, and got a bit overexcited when one was finally on the way. Although Mr Wigg had quite firmly suggested she should let them choose their own colours – they hadn't known yet whether Lachlan was to be a boy or a girl – she had gone right ahead and bought an enormous tin of aqua paint.

To her credit, their daughter-in-law had been very polite, and somehow organised to exchange it for a lovely pale citrus green, which was more than Mr Wigg had ever been able to manage. He and his son had had a good laugh about it all but the daily visits had stopped shortly afterwards.

'Not going up today?' he'd asked.

She had made her lips thin. 'No.'

'Why is that, love?'

'They are *too busy* with the nursery and so on.'

Mr Wigg had put down the basket of eggs, lemons and zucchini he had picked for her to take up. 'Maybe tomorrow, then?'

'Maybe.'

# Custard and Quince

The quince had finally turned rose pink. They had been on the stove the better part of the day, filling the house with their perfume. Mr Wigg left the lid off to allow the syrup to reduce. He had already made his custard and put it in the fridge to cool. It was a dessert you had to plan some way ahead.

His wife had loved custard. She would eat it with a teaspoon, eyes closed. Once, when she had been pregnant – it must have been with his daughter because their son was already running around – she had consumed a whole batch in an afternoon and they had had to have ice-cream with the quince instead. He had found no bowl, only the little teaspoon, licked clean, and the blue serving dish in the sink.

Mr Wigg blew across the wooden spoon to cool the syrup. Neither of his children had appreciated stewed quince, considering it homely and old-fashioned. That pretty much summed him up, too, he supposed. Indeed, he was not unlike a quince: round and lumpy.

For Mr Wigg, the smell of quince cooking was most exotic, conjuring up images of coloured lanterns, pyramid-shaped piles of spices, and rug-lined tents. His son and daughter-in-law, he noticed, had not planted the quince tree he gave them. If he remembered, he would suggest young Traubner add a few quince trees to the orchard. With their wine palates, they might enjoy them. Quince wine was meant to be delicious, too, rather like dessert wine.

He supposed the Traubners knew the whole saga. Although coming from out of town, plenty of folk would have felt obliged to fill them in on all the 'history' once they heard they were buying the place.

Handing over the farm should have been a simple thing. It was in his day. No one asked him or his brothers if they wanted to be farmers; it was just the way it was. Herb hadn't even turned eighteen when he inherited his own place. In some ways not much changed. They had all still turned up for their mother's roast on Sundays and helped each other out at harvest and shearing time.

If he'd had a sister things might have been quite different around home, but she would probably have married another farmer and moved away.

Mr Wigg thought they had come up with quite a good arrangement for his daughter. It only seemed fair; their son had worked the place since he was fifteen, younger even. And it wasn't like she had shown any interest in the property after she left. Turned out she didn't see it quite the same way.

'It's prehistoric, Dad.'

Mr Wigg sighed. 'There are practical considerations when it comes to family and property, these things don't change.'

'Just because something has always been done that way doesn't make it right,' she said. 'It's blatant sexism.' She'd let her hair grow long again, which normally suited her but today her face was almost the same shade of red. 'Out there in the real world, women are fighting for equal pay.'

Mr Wigg blinked. He had been all for her going back to school and on to college but it seemed to make her angrier than ever. 'Will you at least sit down? Try to have a proper conversation,' he said. 'You've upset your mother.'

His daughter pulled a face. 'I don't want to sit down.'

'We'll help you and Lowndes buy a house. I know the money doesn't go far with those city prices but it's all we've got.' The Norris bloke hadn't lasted, of course, took off when Xavier was still too young to remember him. The new fella was decent enough, taking on someone else's boy, and then the twins, but they'd done it tough, he supposed.

'I have three children to support. I have to *work* for a living.'

'If you're suggesting your brother doesn't work hard, you should spend a bit more time here and see what goes on.'

'You don't know what hard work is,' she said. 'And I want half. I'm entitled.'

Mr Wigg ate his quince and custard reading *Orchards from Around the World*, which Lachlan and Fiona had given him for Christmas. His favourite so far was an ancient walnut farm in Kyrgyzstan surrounded by dry stone walls. The trees' gnarled trunks reached up into a tangled canopy, and the farmers' hands were all stained black. Their wives' faces were dark and wrinkled, rather like walnuts themselves.

Tonight a picture of peeled, flattened and dried persimmons, stacked up like little sugared donuts, had caught his eye. He ran his finger stump along the caption. 'Hosh . . . Hoshigaki.' He had never considered drying persimmons, figured there wouldn't be much left after you took all the water out. These Japanese persimmons were hung outside from strings on a bamboo pole – like lines of orange lanterns under all the village's eaves – over a few weeks. The book said they had been doing it that way for seven hundred years. It wouldn't work here, of course; the flies would ruin them and the birds would carry off what was left. He could just see Mrs Wigg's face if he had suggested it.

They might fare a bit better in the fruit dryer though.

# Up the Hill

Mr Wigg set off up the hill. He wanted to see his orchard again before the last of the autumn colours disappeared. The shower of rain overnight had drawn rich scents out of the earth. He took his wife's walking stick, partly for company, but also to steady himself on the uneven ground once it got a bit steep.

He stopped to open a gate, hanging the stick on his arm while he unlatched it. His son's cattle had rubbed the post smooth, better than any fine sanding job you could do. They'd learned how to open the gate, too, after a few years. He and Mrs Wigg had woken to the sound of cattle bellowing in the orchard and leapt out of bed quicker than they had for years to shoo them out. Mrs Wigg had yelled '*hupp hupp*' and clapped her hands with her usual authority, though he knew she was afraid of the steers' horns. They managed to get them out before too much damage was done and enjoyed their eggs and bacon all the more for the exercise.

His son had made a cattle-proof latch the next day and it never happened again. It was almost Wigg-proof now; he struggled to extract the chain from its slot with his stiff old hands. He turned at the sound of a vehicle: young Traubner.

'I'm just going up to cut some thistles. Want a lift?'

Mr Wigg nodded and waited for the boy to drive through. Had he been coming up anyway, or seen him walk by and worried he wouldn't make it up the hill? He had moved quickly if that was it. Mr Wigg shut the gate behind them and climbed into the cab.

'Nice bit of rain last night.'

'I heard it start, then slept like a baby.'

Young Traubner smiled. He dropped the ute back into four-wheel drive as they hit the rocky ground. 'You plant these trees up here?'

Mr Wigg shook his head. 'Whole place was covered in dense scrub once, and big trees like this. Cleared most of them off to farm it,' he said. 'They're ironbarks. And that big one off to the side, that's a stringybark.'

'Dad said there was gold here, back in the day.'

'A seven-mile vein, one of the richest around,' he said. 'There were some old mines just over the back of this hill – where all the Cyprus pines start – but my son filled them in; his cattle kept falling in and breaking their legs or worse.' Mr Wigg gripped the handle on the roof as they lurched over an embankment. 'Someone found a big nugget only a few years ago, ploughing near a track made from old tailings,' he said. 'Was a bit of a dispute about who owned it, from memory. The bloke who found it, the grader who left it there, the bloke who owned the land, or the fellow who owned the mine it originally came from.'

'Is that right?' Young Traubner said. 'I'll have to pay more attention when I'm driving around.' He pulled up in the shade of the largest ironbark, which had, for many years, been home to a wedgetail eagle. The messy nest was deserted now, its sticks weathered and old, falling away in places.

Mr Wigg climbed out, steadying himself on the door. Young Traubner was already striding off with his hoe and shovel.

Mr Wigg made his way up to the boulder he liked to sit on. They had come up here for picnics when the children were young: roast chicken sandwiches with potato salad and lettuce, and cold perry. Afterwards he and his wife would lie on the chequered blanket, sometimes snooze holding hands, while the children chased each other between the trees and made up miniature lands.

When they came back, worn out and tired, they'd all have tea and his wife's fresh lamingtons on the boulder. He would point things out, see if they could pick the Martin's windmill, or Walmersley's shearing shed. In those days you couldn't see the town marching outward, things seemed to stay as still as a late autumn's day.

His orchard was splendid. A full palate of colour, from green through to red and off to brown. The persimmons were obvious, in the middle, calling out for his attention even up here. The others, though more subtle, were as beautiful. He picked them out, one by one.

'You have the best orchard, Mr Wigg.'

Mr Wigg turned. The boy had finished the burrs already, and stood with the shovel on his shoulder.

'Ours is coming along, but you've got a bit of a start on us.'

His son and daughter-in-law had put in an apricot, some apples, plums, and a lemon but got too busy with the feedlot to do much more. 'Takes time, developing a proper orchard,' he said. 'But you get back what you put in. You'd know that. With your grapes.'

'I think I've kidded Dad to let me put in some peaches this winter,' he said. 'Wouldn't mind talking to you about what sort and where best to plant 'em.'

Mr Wigg smiled. 'Bill Spies sells the best ones. Just give me a hoy when you're ready to go get them,' he said. 'I'll make sure he doesn't rip you off.'

# Pomme

The Granny Smiths were just starting to turn a dull yellow. He had been cooking with them for a while – apple sauce with his pork chops and apple and mulberry crumble – but they were at their best for eating about now, the sugars reaching their peak. He had filled two fruit boxes to put away in the pantry for winter. The rest he would leave on the tree.

The Granny Smith was the most ordinary and yet most extraordinary fruit. One of the few originating in Australia and exported to the rest of the world. 'Granny' Maria Ann Smith had been a great orchardist. What would become the Granny Smith, though, was a chance seedling, popping up near a creek on her farm at Eastwood, near Sydney, in 1868. They reckoned it was a hybrid of the European wild apple and the domestic apple.

Poor old Granny died before her apple became a commercial variety but others continued cultivating it. Mr

Wigg's mother had told him that even after he was born, the orchards of Eastwood supplied Granny Smith apples for all of Sydney, when most other varieties had failed. Of course there were no apples grown there now, just buildings, and apples were trucked in from inland and down south.

Up at the old farm, the cook had mostly run the kitchen, but his mother had liked to bake. Her apple pies were magnificent, with a big, high sugary crust. Those were wonderful afternoons, her crisp white apron, hair tied back, the warmth of the wood stove – twice as big as the one he had now – and the perfume of browning pastry.

He realised, when he had his own children, that some of it had been for his benefit, to teach him to cook. Not that she spent as much time with his brothers. He wondered whether she had thought he was different to start with, or if she had encouraged his interest in the orchard and kitchen. Reading, too. She didn't, after all, have any daughters. Perhaps, like most things, it was a mixture of genetics and growing conditions.

Mr Wigg slid the apples under the bottom shelf in the pantry. His wife had liked to eat a Granny Smith after dinner, cut into thin slices with a little knife as she read or, in later years, watched television. She barely made a crunch, or spilled any juices, whereas he needed a plate and towel for the job.

He swiped his finger along the shelf. There was a thin layer of dust over surfaces, jars and bottles, left behind by the summer's dust storms. He should clean it all up, but then it wasn't like anybody was going to see it. The electrician, maybe, when he got him back.

'What are we going to make today, Poppy?'

'I thought we'd make apple pie.'

'Told you,' Lachlan said.

Fiona shook her head, blonde pigtails flicking. 'I said apple pie. *You* said apple tart.'

'Same thing.'

'No it's not.'

'Now, now,' Mr Wigg said. 'Who is going to get me some apples so we can get started?'

Fiona ran off, skidding in her pink ankle socks.

'Do you remember how to make the pastry?'

'Think so,' Lachlan said, taking the mixing bowl.

Fiona returned balancing five apples against her chest, their green skins at odds with her purple-striped shirt. 'Poppy?'

'Yes, love.'

'You need to clean your pantry. It's very dusty.'

Mr Wigg blinked and took the apples one by one. 'Oh, do you want to clean it for me?'

'I can't reach!'

'True.'

'We can help you do it, maybe,' Lachlan said. 'With the ladder.'

Mr Wigg smiled. 'Next time. We've got cooking to do.'

'Can I skin the apples?' Fiona had the peeler at the ready and Lachlan was rubbing butter into flour. Mr Wigg sat down at the kitchen table to rest his legs.

Lachlan looked over his shoulder. 'Dad said you used to play cricket, too.'

Mr Wigg rubbed at his face. 'I haven't told you about the cricket matches we used to have up at the old farm?'

'*No*,' Lachlan said, as if it was a grand omission on Mr Wigg's part. He'd started playing for the local under-twelves and apparently took it very seriously, practising his bowling against the wall of the shed at the new place.

'We had our own pitch. All the gear was kept in a wooden box under the pepper tree. The sort of box they used to ship rifles in but that's a whole other story. Every Sunday there'd be a match. We'd mow the field, roll the pitch, and put on our whites.'

'Who'd you play?'

'There were a whole lot of district teams, Seven Mile, that was us – made up of four Wiggs, three O'Donnels, Johnson, and . . . a couple of others who I can no longer remember. There was Emu Creek, Chalkers Crossing, Bellthorpe, Moppity Road, and the town teams. Friendly matches mind you, but it got pretty competitive towards the end of the season.'

'Were you a batter or a bowler?'

'I was a better batsman,' he said. 'My brother James was the bowler in the family. Although I didn't mind having a trundle now and then.'

'Was Seven Mile the best team?'

'We did okay. Won a few years. Then the Snedden boys started playing for Emu Creek. Five of them and all over six-foot-six. Won every year for a while,' Mr Wigg said. 'Seven Mile were legendary in my dad's day, but then they had Smithy.'

'Who's Smithy?' Fiona said, holding up a long, springing curl of apple skin for approval.

Mr Wigg boggled his eyes, making her giggle. 'He was our blacksmith up at the old farm. He shoed the horses and made wheels for the wagons, pots and gate hinges, and all sorts of things.'

'Did he make pokers, Poppy?' Lachlan said. 'Like you?'

Mr Wigg smiled. 'He did. But he was much better at it than me; he made magic at that anvil. And as you'd expect, he was as strong as an ox with absolutely *enormous* hands,' Mr Wigg said. 'From pumping the bellows and wielding big hammers. Smithy was our wicket keeper because he could catch anything, with or without gloves, but well, could he *bat*. He'd hit the ball so far sometimes it couldn't be found. I was about your age then, Lachlan, and I'd be sent off into the long grass to look for the damn thing while the players had a drinks break.'

Lachlan frowned. 'What if you couldn't find it?'

'We'd just get another one,' he shrugged. 'One time he hit a straight drive, right down into the pepper tree, by the dam. It got lodged up there, or snagged on something, and one of the opposition's outfielders had time enough to run down, stand underneath, and catch it when it dropped free.'

Lachlan turned. 'And he was out?'

'On ninety-nine,' Mr Wigg said. 'Unlucky.'

'I *reckon*,' Lachlan said, shaking his head.

Fiona started slicing apples with the big knife. Mr Wigg got up from the table. 'That's it, make sure you cut away from your hand there.'

'Is this thin enough?' Lachlan said.

Mr Wigg checked the pastry. 'You could roll it a touch more, then pop it in the dish and I'll help you trim it off.'

'What about you, Poppy? What was the coolest thing you ever did?' Lachlan said.

'The first game I ever played – I was only fourteen or so – was because my Uncle Earl had ripped open his hand on the harvester the evening before an important match against Emu Creek. My brother was older, but they needed a batsman, so my dad asked me to fill in,' he said. 'I didn't sleep a wink the night before. Emu Creek had this fast bowler who had been terrorising the district that summer. Flash, we called him.'

Lachlan frowned as a bit of the pastry tore off during the journey from bench to dish.

'It's all right, we'll just push it back together, like this.'

Fiona tugged at his trousers. 'Do I put the apples on now?'

'Have you added the sugar?' He waited until Fiona emptied the measuring cup over the sliced apples and then carried the saucepan over to the stove.

'So,' Lachlan said. 'How'd you go?'

Mr Wigg smiled. 'I came in at number five; we were struggling a bit. But Smithy and I turned it around. I scored fifty-nine runs. I hit that Flash all round the ground,' he said. 'Mind you, the others had already taken the shine off the ball. But still. We won the game. My dad was actually pleased with me, kept slapping me on the back and telling the story over and over. Gave me my first beer.' Mr Wigg searched his pockets for a hanky and blew his nose.

'Dad's like that,' Lachlan said. 'It takes a fair bit to impress him. But if he says something's good, you know it really is.'

# Blood and Bone

Mr Wigg forked blood and bone into the earth beneath his white peaches. A southerly had the last of the autumn leaves floating down around him. The nights were getting cooler, too. When he'd come out first thing to pee under the lemon tree, everything had been a bit brisk.

He could've stopped in bed longer, of course, but sometimes you just wanted the night over. The first few months after his wife died, he had struggled to sleep right up until first light, then woken up late, sick with remembering. Something about the dark had all your worst thoughts getting the better of you.

*'Blood is blood and bone is bone, we've got to feed if full fruit is to be grown.'* The yellow peaches, nectarines and apricots all joined in, assuming they'd be next. It was a slow song, the trees winding down as winter crept closer. There was

none of the warmer weather's heckling or boasting, their energy now turning inwards instead.

He could hear the drone of tractors in the distance: real farmers at work. His son would be ploughing, too, at the new place. Although there was less ground to cover, it would be trickier with the steep slope and rocks.

Mr Wigg had ploughed the orchard a few weeks earlier, after the first bit of rain. It took about as long for him to do his few acres with his old Ford as it did the blokes over the hill to finish several hundred. He had more trees to work around in a smaller space, and it wasn't as if he was in any hurry. And they had their flash new machines.

His wife had preferred the orchard grassed and mown. It looked nice most of the year, it was true, but in summer the rye grass soon got out of control and all that competition wasn't in the fruit trees' best interests.

Mr Wigg was slower to get going again in the afternoon. He tried to gee the trees up with the blood and bone song, singing it deep and slow like 'Sweet Chariot' but they only managed a hum in response.

He ferried blood and bone back and forth, worked it in. Kept an eye on the clouds building. The queen's gardener, no doubt, had a dozen or so apprentices to do all the heavy work. With orchards that size, they'd need a horse and cart, too, for hauling things around.

His son and daughter used to like pushing the barrow for

him, fighting over it usually, but sometimes working together, one on each side. After a time they would grow bored, as children do, and he'd turn around to find they had left their posts to climb a tree or throw clods at each other. He figured that was all right, as long as they were having fun outside.

Planting was their favourite chore. They would gear up in gum boots and hats, and drag a shovel behind them, although they were not up to much digging. They could stamp down the earth though, and water in the trees, and in that way the orchard was theirs, too.

Traubner's ute pulled up by the fence. Mr Wigg leaned his fork against the wheelbarrow and walked over. Dry leaves rustled on the trees behind him.

'Afternoon, Mr Wigg.'

They shook hands over the fence.

'We're going to have to do some spraying over the next few days,' Traubner said. 'We'll do it first thing, when it's nice and still, but there might be a bit of drift.'

They would be trying to get rid of the Paterson's curse, he expected. And the rye grass. Grapes needed full run of the soil. 'That'll be fine,' Mr Wigg said. His daughter-in-law was always going on about chemical sprays, especially on foods, but he'd been drenched in the stuff plenty of times when he was a young bloke. She reckoned there was a link between sprays and Parkinson's, but surely every farmer around would have it if that were true.

He had read the articles she gave him though, which made a lot of sense, and had cut back on what he used on the fruit. Let the insects and birds do what they were meant to. It took a bit more work but it wasn't as if he lacked the time. It was probably his imagination, but the peaches seemed to have developed even more flavour over the last few years.

Traubner lifted his head towards the workshop. 'I hear you're a master blacksmith?'

'I give it a go. Nothing too fancy.'

'That's the European blood coming out, you know; old village craft,' Traubner said. 'They're trying to revive those skills back home, makes sure they are passed on. Maybe you can teach Andy a thing or two; I'm useless with tools.'

'Of course,' Mr Wigg said. 'I could do that.'

As much as he'd tried, Mr Wigg hadn't been able to sort things out with his daughter. His son had tried to reason with her, shown her all the figures. Explained the farm would be useless split in two – barely supporting a family as it was – and that he couldn't buy her out. His son had again offered to pay her deposit on a house, prepared to borrow some money to give her a more generous amount, but nothing seemed to appease her.

It was a re-creation of the way they had played board games as children, his daughter with her arms crossed and scowling, and his son pleading with her to keep playing. Of course, there was much more at stake now.

She'd gone back to the city without even saying goodbye. Packed her bags and children into the car before dawn and roared up the drive in a cloud of dust.

Mr Wigg's wife hadn't spoken for nearly a week, lay in bed staring at the wall. He hadn't seen her like that since her mother died. He had tiptoed around, eventually getting her up and trying to distract her with custard, new rose catalogues and games of Scrabble.

'Play again?'

'You let me win,' she'd said.

'You always win.'

She had half-smiled. 'True.'

He had put his hand on hers. 'What do you want me to do?'

She had shrugged, scraped the little wooden letters into their bag, and packed up the game. 'I don't know.'

'Are you angry with me, love?'

'Of course not,' she had said, her face angry all the same.

In the end, faced with silence, and no apparent options, he had gone ahead with the handover. It was probably the wrong thing to do, in hindsight. They should have waited. But his son had been in a hurry; the crops needed sowing and a new financial year had been about to begin.

Land passed from one generation to the next, as it always had. Although it marked an ending of sorts, Mr Wigg had settled into his armchair more easily that night, looking forward to seeing all the energy he – and his brothers, father and grandfather – had put into the place over the years somehow renewed.

Of course, as it had taken him almost a lifetime to learn, things seldom turned out the way he intended.

# Winter

# Bellows

Mr Wigg had lit the forge for warmth. Even with all the workshop's windows and doors closed, the cold crept in, fogging his breath and stiffening his joints. Mrs Wigg had liked to sleep in on a winter's morning, the thought of cold lino sending her burrowing back under the blankets. He had never been able to stop in bed long once he woke, and would shuffle out to stoke up the stove and make his own breakfast. Hot tea and a bowl of oats with honey and cream, toast with butter and jam. She didn't approve of the cream, of course, and would not have allowed it were she in the kitchen. She said since he no longer did the work of two men, he needed only to eat for one. It was true he'd had to let his belt out a few notches over the years. After she died, there was no one to watch what he ate.

He cut boards into lengths for a new vegetable bed, and repaired a shovel handle with a clamp, glue and screws. His hands weren't so good today, trembling like some palsy-ridden fool's, and what was left of his fingers were fat and clumsy; he had to go slow, and even then he was unsteady.

He gathered up wood scraps from around the bench and threw them into the fire, rubbing his hands together over the flames for warmth. A few strokes of its long wooden handle and the forge was breathing again, the bellows blowing the coals red hot. The wood soon burned away. Outside, the paddocks were still white with frost.

Mr Wigg cleared tools and bits and pieces from the top of the anvil and dusted it off with the rag he kept tucked in his back pocket. All the while he pulled on the handle in a steady rhythm, his hand resting easy on the edge, the spot worn smooth by many men's palms.

He gathered together his hammers, tongs, and pliers, and checked that the other tools were all in their spots close by. Now he pumped the handle a little harder; you needed a white hot fire to shape iron.

The forge he had built himself, before he and his brothers started on the house, but the bellows had come from the shop up at the old farm. The anvil, too. They had both travelled out on the boat with his grandfather, having already served their time in a village he had never seen.

Up at the old farm, in the mining village's heyday, Smithy had worked six days a week, shoeing horses and making and repairing tools. As a boy, Mr Wigg would wander down after school, barefoot, to fill the water bucket and fetch fresh wood. Sometimes, Smithy had let him hold lengths of iron on the anvil while he hammered with both hands, the muscles on his sweaty arms bulging out of his shirt. When Smithy gave the sign, young Mr Wigg would plunge the iron into the water to cool with a hiss. The huffing of the forge, clanging of metal on metal and hissing and spitting led him to imagine himself in a dragon's lair, or under a mountain making magical swords with the dwarves. Silly boy's stuff.

As he grew older, when he wasn't fencing or shooting foxes or on some other job his father or uncles had given him, he'd be down there helping Smithy. Eventually, Smithy let him shoe his own horse and do some of the easier jobs. Once he grew tall, with the shoulders and arms of a man to be, and Smithy's back went, Mr Wigg had taken over the role of striker, wielding the big hammer while Smithy held the iron.

He'd learned all the basics by the time the shop shut down. Smithy went somewhere else, another town. Doing exhibition work for a historical village.

At dinner one night, a few years later – roast spring pork with noisy crackling – his father had mentioned he'd been to Smithy's funeral that afternoon. Mr Wigg had put down his knife and fork and asked to be excused. He'd never even known Smithy's real name – surely it couldn't actually be Smith – but he had spent almost as much time with him as his father and would have liked to have had a chance to say goodbye.

With his free hand, Mr Wigg pulled a length of quarter-inch from the rack on the wall and plunged it into the fire.

When it had taken on the same bright white–red as the coals, he held it firm on the anvil, placed the cutter against it and hit it once, hard, with the hammer, splitting the end in two. He rolled it over and repeated the process. Four even pieces of red hot iron splayed out from the top. He pushed it back into the coals to soften again.

Mr Wigg hurried over to the vice and clamped the top edge of the split pieces. Using the pliers, and his gloved hand to hold it level, he twisted hard one hundred and eighty degrees to form a convex spiralling handle. He plunged it into the water bucket to 'quench' what was left of the heat. Next he worked to weld the top end back together, and hammered it into a ball, like a cumquat.

The fancy stuff he'd had to teach himself, over the years, from books and exhibition smiths. He had set about making wrought-iron gates for the top of the driveway, complete with scrolls and sheaves of wheat, which was all far too ambitious for his level of skill at that stage. Mrs Wigg had been impressed, though, giving them three coats of premium white paint to match their sign. He had got out the binoculars just to make sure there wasn't a can of aqua hidden anywhere.

Now he sharpened the other end of the piece of iron, hammering out one side and then the other into a long point, like a spear. These pokers sold like hot cakes at the craft centre. Well they used to, before Mrs Wigg died. And probably would again, unless some other old bugger was making them now.

He bent another piece of iron into a tight curve over the heel of the anvil, cooled it, and set about welding it on above the sharpened end of the poker – heating the two areas and hammering them together while soft – to form the hook you needed to move the wood about in the fire. He heated the spot above the weld, laid the poker lengthways in the vice and used the twisting clamp to turn in a decorative twist. The final touch was his stamp; he heated the stem just below the handle, set the poker down on the anvil and gave the punch a firm tap with the hammer: *wigg*.

# Persimmon Sill

**M**r Wigg sharpened his razor and lathered up. Shaving always seemed more difficult in winter, the bathroom cold and the mirror inclined to fog. He stretched his skin smooth – as smooth as it would go these days – and cut downwards, trying to steady his arm against his chest. He should be grateful he could still grow whiskers, he supposed, one of the few markers of manhood he had left. The hair on his head was as good as gone and everything else hung too far to the south, next to useless.

He gave himself a couple of nicks on the upward strokes under his chin, which was nothing unusual, but they bled into his shirt collar. It was probably time to try the electric shaver his son had given him. The razor gave a closer shave, and he was fond of the ritual of it all, but you needed a steady hand to hold an open blade to your throat every morning.

He washed up and shuffled into the warmth of the kitchen, the heels of his slippers scuffing the lino. Outside, the lawn was frozen white. He measured oats and water into a saucepan and put them on to boil. It was morbid, but he always felt closer to death in winter; everything was slower and more difficult, bleached of colour.

He dragged the big old kettle onto the heat, gave his porridge a stir and spooned tea leaves into the pot. It was nice to take his time over breakfast, at least, with not much he could do outside until the sun warmed things through. He scraped his porridge into a bowl and covered it with brown sugar, letting it melt a little before he added the milk.

It was only last winter that his wife died. Each day seemed to have passed slowly but somehow not add up to a year, looking back. As if there were pieces missing.

She had seemed fine that day, better than she had been for weeks, eating most of her dinner and beating him at Scrabble by nearly two hundred points. She had used all seven letters not just once but twice: for 'ministry' and 'gluteals'. He'd challenged that last one, but when he flicked over the page in the dictionary, there it was: buttocks, of all things.

When he woke at half past five, the birds stirring and chattering in the eaves, the light shafting in all golden, she was gone.

It was mid-morning when he put on his red parka and beanie and headed out to the orchard. There was still a little frost in the lee side of the furrows and the fog hadn't yet burned off. His peach and apricot trees stood naked and silent.

The persimmons had shed all their leaves, too, but rich orange globes hung from their bare branches. Mr Wigg lifted the net and picked off the darkest of them until he had filled an ice-cream container. At this time of year, the persimmon trees were rather smug, all too aware of their own beauty. They liked to remind him of the quality not just of their fruit but of their slender, silver-grey limbs. Part of the well-regarded ebony family, their timber had once been used to make piano keys. This was a subject best not to mention, unless you were prepared to listen to long tales of injustice and persecution. In Asia, their timber was still used for panelling and cabinets, and in America for pool cues and traditional longbows. He didn't dare tell the persimmons any of this, of course, though the idea of a longbow held a certain appeal. He led them to believe such permanent harvesting was a thing of the past, and that one of the attractions of life in a new country was leaving all that history behind. Mr Wigg gave the trees a final admiring glance and carried the fruit inside.

He lined the persimmons up on the windowsill, upside down, to ripen. Sun on the glass reflected orange into the kitchen. There was, after all, plenty of colour left in the world, even in winter.

# Branch and Twig

Mr Wigg opened his sketchbook at the peach tree pages. After months of fiddling, he was finally happy. He had added in the leaves and fruit on one side, and left it bare on the other.

Underneath, he worked on an iron translation, breaking it down into separate components as he figured how he might make them. He was using the book his wife had given him, ordered in especially from England (though written by a German, he noticed now) after his daughter left home. To try to keep him busy, he had realised even at the time.

It set out all the traditional methods, with diagrams and photographs and lists of tools. He wished now he'd used it more when his wife was around, to show her how much he'd appreciated it. But that was the way of things in a marriage; you always thought you had plenty of time for everything. When you looked back, regrets, the things left unsaid, were the hardest to live with.

Mr Wigg blew his nose and stuffed his hanky back in his pocket. His scrolling branches spread out from the central trunk. Leaves curled down and the fruit shone like globes. He made a box leading off from each piece with a more detailed diagram.

It had been the old gardener up home who had taught him how to see the shape of a tree, how to plan from the outset, nurture and encourage it to be the best it could be. It was like sculpture, he used to say, with what you cut away as important as what you left behind.

Mr Wigg hadn't appreciated until years later, after his own orchard was well-established, how much energy Jack must have put in to an orchard that was not his, working for a future his family would not enjoy.

Jack used to say that a good orchard was like a well-lived life. The one up at the old farm, with its hundred-year-old pears leaning over the entrance gates, held more Wigg history than anything written down. There'd been birthday parties and weddings, hot Christmases, family portraits, good harvests and bad. His brother even reckoned they had a lost sibling buried beneath the youngest apricot, a girl who had died at birth. It was probably rubbish, but his mother had been awfully fond of the tree and it always fruited better than all the others. You didn't ask about those sorts of things in those days, and now it was too late.

He'd walked through the old orchard, in the weeks before it was sold. Wished he could take it all with him somehow.

There was a lot of Jack there, although he was long since dead; an orchard takes on the character of those who tend it. His mother was there, too, and their cook, picking into wooden tubs carried on their hips. Climbing ladders in their long dresses and white aprons.

He'd seen traces of himself as a young man, in some of the more youthful trees grown too close together, and pruned too gently.

Of course, it had been let go by then, his brother not having the time or the interest. His brother's wife had used the fruit – she had a sweet tooth that saw her become quite round – but didn't tend the trees.

Sometimes he wondered if there was one moment, one intersection, offering up another path in life. How things turned out was partly out of your hands, but what if that one chance slipped by unnoticed? If Mr Wigg had been the elder son, the old orchard would have been his. Perhaps he would have had the courage then to expand it, do something different. Be more prosperous. He sighed. Most likely he would have felt more pressure to make it as a farmer, taking his yields from wheat and wool.

Mr Wigg pumped the bellows, slow and steady. He'd built up quite a fire, partly to warm the workshop – there was another heavy frost this morning – and partly to work with the larger pieces of iron. The flames had the dragon's roar that had drawn him to the forge as a boy.

He attached the scroll jig to the anvil, dropping its stem into the square hole. With both hands, he lifted the piece of iron and nestled the top third into the coals. When it was white hot, he took it out, and worked to take the corners down, hammering each edge, turning and hammering, turning and hammering until the top end was round and slightly tapered. He returned it to the heat.

Now he hooked the hot iron into the jig and, gripping it by the cooler end, walked it around the anvil to bend it into a scroll, curving gently back into the centre of the piece of iron. Mr Wigg lifted it off, lowered it in the water – he'd had to fill the half-barrel for the larger process – and heated the other end.

For the bottom end, he left it square but repeated the scrolling process in reverse to form a long s-shaped branch. The iron hissed as he quenched for the final time. Mr Wigg laid the first branch out on the floor. 'Well.'

He worked to make another, this time scrolling a little more loosely. He laid it out on the floor beside the other and stood back. 'Not bad.'

Mr Wigg hammered and bent another three main branches. These had only one scroll, arching back to their base. By lunchtime, the shape of the peach tree was fanned out on the workshop floor.

Mr Wigg put away his tools, shut the door behind him and walked up to the house. A currawong warbled from the clothesline. The sky was clear but the breeze bit at his face after the warmth of the forge.

He made a corned-beef sandwich with pickled beetroot, and ate it with a cup of tea in the kitchen.

Mr Wigg's arms and shoulders ached the next day but he was back at the forge soon after breakfast. It was a bit like the day after the first cricket match of the summer, you needed to keep moving through the pain and, ideally, do it all again. For the smaller branches, he used half-inch and quarter-inch, breaking the corners down almost to the base. These he shaped by hand, hammering the tapered ends over the edge of the anvil and tapping the tips into fantastic shapes.

Each one was slightly different, bending this way and that, turning out or in. Some of the finer pieces he curled around and around the anvil's horn, in a spiral. These would bear the tree's leaves.

Smithy would have been impressed with his free work; he had always sneered at patterns and jigs. When he was a boy, Smithy had had him make nail after nail, by hand, until they each came out almost identical. Mr Wigg bought nails at the hardware store now, like everyone else, which was much more practical, of course. There was something about a handmade nail, though. Something infinitely pleasing. Mr Wigg still had a couple of the nails he had made as a boy, and one of Smithy's he'd used as a template, on the sill of the workshop window.

It was drizzling today, giving it the look of the English countryside outside. Almost. If it weren't for the ironbarks watching on from up on the hill.

Mr Wigg's hammer sounded on the anvil like the village bell, each stroke sending off a spray of burning sparks. He beat on, shaping the branches of the tree that had come to him in his dreams.

# Citrus

Frost crunched under his boots. Traubner's grape trellises, all strung now, were dark lines across white paddocks. After next winter the vines' pruned-back branches would start squirling along the cold wires. In Europe, he'd read, vines could survive months of snow, storing energy in their roots and wood until the soil warmed up. A robin redbreast landed on the fence wire, chest puffed, as if setting his colourful self in the frame. Mr Wigg laughed and watched him till he flew off in pursuit of an insect.

He turned back to his own orchard, his citrus corner almost as impressive with its dark foliage and orange and yellow fruit. They were the gangs of four: four orange trees and four lemons, squaring off against each other like courtiers from opposing houses. The oranges were much larger trees, but the thorny Lisbon lemons were the more formidable.

The dimpled skin of the oranges was cold on his fingers. Mr Wigg dropped them into the plastic bucket at his feet, the first few making a loud *thunk*. Although the little folded-over hole in their skin could be argued to be a human trait, the marker of a sentient being, the oranges were very sensitive about their fruit's 'navel' and the lemons knew it. It was actually the mark of mutation, a second, smaller orange forming at the base of the first, like a conjoined twin. The lemons, always quick to cut to the chase, latched onto the 'mutant' aspect of the story.

The oranges cast their shadows over the lemons and sang of tapestries and poems and *orangeries* but, as the bitter lemons would always point out, the oranges in those tapestries did not have navels.

The Lisbon Lemons made much of their breeding from an old Portuguese line via the orange groves of California. They put on silly accents that sounded more French than Portuguese. In the end, the oranges fell back on their sweetness and lack of seeds. They had only to gesture to Mr Wigg's bucket, as he walked back towards the house: piled high with oranges, with only two lemons on top.

Mr Wigg juiced oranges until he had filled the small glass jug. He added two tablespoons of sugar and stirred it in. His son was always giving him a hard time about adding sugar or salt, especially when Fiona and Lachlan were here, but he didn't see the harm. He poured himself a glass and drank it in three gulps. There was nothing like orange juice straight from the tree. Refrigerated to just the right temperature by nature herself.

His son said that in the tropics oranges were not orange at all but green. The orange pigment in their skin came from higher chilling hours, which they did not get near the equator. What was the word for the colour orange, then, in those languages? It was strange to think about.

He opened the stove door, warmed his hands, and attached two pieces of white bread to his toasting fork. He singed them on both sides and pushed them off onto a plate with his finger stump. He took the squashiest persimmon from the window sill, pulled off its cap-like stalk and squeezed the pulp out over his toast; jam in a skin. His wife had never been that keen on persimmons but he loved their delicate sweetness. He poured his tea and set himself up at the table with yesterday's newspaper.

He checked the death notices first. At his age, friends just kept dropping off, especially in winter. People didn't always think to call and tell him anymore; his wife had kept up with things for both of them.

Old Paul Needham's son had died, hit in the chest with a rock from a lawnmower. People thought he'd been shot at first, reckoned they'd heard gunfire. There had been a big investigation but it turned out there was something wrong with his heart. Only forty bloody years old.

Blacky from bowls had passed away, another one gone to cancer. There'd be a big turnout for that on Tuesday. Some of his war mates were still around and Blacky had been the sort of fellow who always bought the first round and kept them all laughing. Mr Wigg took off his glasses to wipe his face. It would almost be better to die first than have to go to so many funerals.

His first funeral had been his father's. He and his brothers had carried the coffin out of the church with their uncles in stiff suits; a family regiment of almost the same height. They were all gone now, too, and there weren't many left who remembered them, the old farm or how things used to be.

It frustrated him at times, but he couldn't really recall his wife's funeral; he had sat up the front with his son and daughter, their families either side. At the graveside, someone had put a hand on his shoulder and he'd realised, with a horrible rush, he would never touch his wife again.

# Leaf and Stem

**M**r Wigg dropped his first attempt in the water bucket. It made a wet *plonk* as it hit the bottom. He stretched his back and, with a weak *toot*, he let off some of the wind that was making him uncomfortable. Too much cucumber, perhaps.

'What are you making?'

Mr Wigg turned. It was a hazard not being able to hear people approach anymore. His son was leaning in the doorway of the workshop. 'Nothing much.'

'Looks like something.' His son stepped into the gloom and picked up a branch. He ran his fingers over the joins and pushed his eyebrows up into his forehead. 'How'd you get this finish?'

Mr Wigg wiped his face with his hanky, folded it and put it back in his pocket. Shuffled forward a little. 'You stretch it as you twist it. Then flatten it out with a ball hammer,' he said. 'It's not finished yet.'

'What's it for?'

Mr Wigg shrugged.

His son laughed, that little snort under his breath that probably meant he thought his father was wasting his time again.

'There are some oranges, lemons and eggs by the back step if you'd like them.'

'Thanks,' he said. 'We had scrambled eggs this morning. Fiona kept exclaiming how yellow they are.'

'Carotenoids,' Mr Wigg said. 'You have to give them plenty of fresh stuff: greens.'

'I'll tell her that,' his son said. 'I brought your mail down. There's a parcel.'

'Right. Thanks.'

'I've rung up about the forms for patenting the fruit dryer,' he said. 'There's a fee, but I'll cover it.'

'There's no need for that.'

'I know, but you've more than repaid us in dried fruit already. Fiona is addicted to dried apricots.'

Mr Wigg smiled. Fiona had always been his wife's favourite, so it made a certain sense. If he had managed to get the dryer done while she had been alive, he was sure she would have been nibbling dried apricots all winter, too. 'Thank you.'

'I'll get onto that bit of guttering next week, okay? Fiona and Lachlan are home sick today.'

'Are they all right?'

'Just a cold. But they're all sniffly and miserable. Marg has them set up in front of the fire watching a movie.'

'Hot lemon drinks are good,' he said. 'That's what we always gave you. Bit of honey and tiny splash of brandy at night.'

His son nodded. 'See you next week, then.'

Mr Wigg watched his son, broad-backed as he bent to pick up the fruit and eggs. *He'd make a good striker.*

When small, his son had spent a lot of time by the forge in winter, staring into the flames and watching how everything was done. Mr Wigg hadn't had the heart to enforce Smithy's rigours on him; it seemed better that the boy enjoyed himself. He had learned how to make hooks and handles, his preference for the practical evident even then. He had flair nonetheless, his hooks deep and bold, curving back like a sickle, and his handles spiralled or scrolled, one even featuring a dragon's head.

Mr Wigg leaned down, hand on the edge of the forge to retrieve his leaf. Held it up to the light coming in through the window. The weight was good, thinning nicely at the edge. And the shape okay. But getting the curve and the centre fold was going to be a challenge. He set it down on the anvil and shook his head. He should probably be out there with the real trees anyway.

He put all the tools back on their hooks and in their slots, pushed the bucket against the wall with his boot. He slid his beanie back on and stepped around the iron branches. In the doorway, he hesitated, went back for the leaf, and slipped it into his pocket.

# Death Lottery

Mr Wigg had meant not to watch it this time, but they sneaked it in right after the news. It was strangely compelling watching the numbers tumble around, determining young men's fates like some sort of roulette. They were saying the war would be over by the end of the year, but they had been saying that for a while and kept on recruiting.

He had thought the last war, in Korea of all places, had dragged on longer than possible, but as it turned out, it had been nothing compared to this.

They had taken in some British boys then, from a ship serving off the coast of Korea. Someone had figured out that long periods of waiting at sea, with a high likelihood of coming under fire at any minute, was not good for the nerves, and that it would be beneficial to give them a break working on a farm. They weren't much use at first, but soon learned to bail hay, herd sheep, and drive the tractor. They had put a new roof on the machinery shed, and helped him build a pergola for his grapes.

Three of them at once they had at one stage, and the boys' eyes nearly fell out of their heads at all the fresh food and a fully stocked pantry. Mr Wigg and his wife had been pleased to fatten them up and teach them a little about the country. They were popular at the pub in town, telling great stories, and falling victim to a few local furphies, too.

He hadn't cared much for all their smoking and drinking, but they had been great with the children. His son took them up into the hills so they could see kangaroos, wallabies and kookaburras, and they came back carrying him on their shoulders as if he had changed their lives somehow.

His daughter had grown quite attached to the youngest fellow, followed him around everywhere. It had been the most interested in the farm she had been for some time. They were part of the family by the time they left – somehow having become both more boyish and more manly – breaking everyone's hearts.

They had all kept in touch though, the boys strangely grateful for the experience. They had written to his wife for years, keeping her up to date with all their news. She wrote back every few months, though leaving out their family dramas towards the end.

One of them had come to the funeral, an old man himself by then, but Mr Wigg had not been able to speak with him at the time. He should have; it was a ridiculous way to come.

And he didn't imagine he would have the opportunity to see the man again.

He got up to throw another log on the fire, and prodded at the coals with the poker. Mrs Wigg had never been able to keep warm in winter; sat with a rug over her knees no matter how he got the fire to blaze. Her arthritis bothered her, curling her fingers and swelling her knuckles in later years. Never stopped her doing anything, but he could tell when it pained her.

He gripped the mantel to straighten up and knocked over a photo frame. When he had his balance again, he righted it. It was of his daughter's children: Xavier, Carolyn and Viv. He'd like to see a bit more of them. It was a shame, too, for Lachlan and Fiona not to know their cousins. Xavier had spent a few holidays here, once he was old enough, to give his mother a break, and they had all played together a few times when Fiona was still a toddler, but probably none of them remembered much.

Mrs Wigg had set up a blow-up pool out in the garden – it had been a hell of a summer that year. They were all shy with each other at first, but eventually came together in play. Xavier was a quiet lad, and although older, a bit softer than Lachlan. They soon got to work emptying the pool Mrs Wigg had taken such pains to fill, employing Fiona with a bucket.

His daughter hadn't visited that often before and wasn't likely to now. Not since the twins were born. Part of him hadn't even expected her at his wife's funeral. He hadn't known what to say to her or her to him, but she had sat close in the church. Held his hand. Didn't hang around for the wake though.

His son's wife said that was a sign of guilt, and there might have been a bit of truth in that. She had just lost her mother though, and that was difficult enough for anyone, whatever the circumstances.

He should probably call, offer to take the train up to the city. People tended to calm down over time. And she could only say no. When it was a bit warmer, perhaps.

He set the box of saplings down in the back of the ute and leaned on the tray to get his breath. If his son had wondered where on earth he was going to plant them, he hadn't asked. Years ago, in one of their dust ups, his son had shouted that there wasn't room for one more food tree on the whole farm.

In any case, he'd picked up the white and yellow peach Mr Wigg has asked for as well as a Portugal quince. He'd made none of the usual jokes about the Americans feeding peaches to the pigs, which Mr Wigg had always found hard to believe. Those Americans either didn't know how to grow peaches or had no sense of taste. And his son liked peaches perfectly well, judging by how many he ate each season. He probably should have waited until young Traubner was ready to go and get the trees together, but they were busy people and always bringing down his mail or mowing the lane for him when he wasn't looking.

Mrs Traubner had stopped in with some fruit wine. To see what he thought, she'd said, but he couldn't help wondering if she was checking whether he could look after the place on his own. She'd said they were thinking about making fruit wines commercially, later on. And liqueurs. To help bring in the tourists. The sample bottle was delicious peach: aromatic and honey sweet. He'd sipped it over ice, as she'd suggested. Perhaps a little too much the first night; he woke up on the floor in front of the fire, which had long gone out.

Mr Wigg had given her a bottle of the perry for Traubner; she'd said she didn't take alcohol herself, which seemed a bit odd for a winegrower's wife.

He went back into the house for the oranges and dried fruit. He had given them a mix of things but was particularly proud of the persimmons. They didn't look much like the Japanese ones – he hadn't had the heart to flatten them – but the sugar had crystallised perfectly on the outside and they tasted wonderful. He had slowed the process down, running the fan on low and turning it off overnight. It was getting pretty cold out on the verandah, and the air was dry, perhaps not so unlike the eaves of a Japanese house.

The ute made the usual fuss about starting; it wasn't as if he could threaten to buy a new one, being unlicensed and all. Not with any credibility, anyway.

He set off up the lane, stopping at the ramp to open a gate and follow the old track up to the Traubner house. Fiona and Lachlan used to tear down this track on Saturdays, or when there was news to bring. His wife had always made sure she had cake or biscuits at the ready 'just in case'. She grumbled about how much those two ate. 'Must have hollow legs,' she'd say. It had given her real pleasure though, to make them treats and hear their stories.

Mrs Traubner opened the back door before he reached the steps but he'd clearly come at a bad time. Her eyes were all puffy and her apron was on inside out.

'I just popped up to leave these for you, Mrs Traubner,' he said. 'I should have rung first.'

'It's fine, Mr Wigg,' she said. 'Won't you come in? We've just put the kettle on.'

Mr Traubner was sitting on a stool by the kitchen bench. He didn't look too good either. Mr Wigg took the chair by the stove. They'd had a hell of a time getting the great thing inside; unbeknown to them, his daughter-in-law had ordered the largest one in the store and they'd already put in the door frames. Mr Wigg had nearly had a heart attack holding up the bottom end while they manoeuvred it around.

'Sorry to just turn up,' he said.

Mrs Traubner pulled down three cups. 'You turn up anytime,' she said. 'I'd like the company.'

Mr Traubner smiled a sad smile. 'It's Andy,' he said. 'He's been drafted. We've just had a bit of a shock.'

*That bloody lottery.* Mr Wigg looked at the floor. He'd thought the boy younger than twenty. He was too young to go off to fight in the jungle, he knew that much. 'I'm sure sorry to hear that,' he said.

'He's gone into town to see the lawyer. To see if there's anything we can do.'

'Can you argue you need him on the farm?' Mr Wigg said.

Traubner shrugged his shoulders. 'He wanted to go off to uni but we kidded him to come over here with us,' he said. 'If he was studying he wouldn't have to go.'

'It's just not right,' Mrs Traubner said. 'Too young to vote, but old enough to be sent off to a war he had no say in.'

Mr Wigg followed the fence line home, letting the ute roll downhill. He was a bit worn out with all the talking. And his bladder was full after too much tea.

He turned up the heater but it only blew cold air.

All the lawyer talk had unsettled him. It bothered him that Andy might have to go off and fight, but he wasn't so sure there was any clever way around it. They didn't think like that in his day. The only time they had really had anything to do with lawyers was the Year Everything Went Wrong and it seemed to him they were a smarmy bunch, making more money than was right out of people who had got themselves upset.

When the fancy letter from their daughter's solicitor had turned up in the mail, he and his wife had sat around the table for an hour or so with tea, trying to make sense of it. In the end, Mrs Wigg had gone and called their son. Their daughter-in-law had had to get him down off the roof. When he arrived, his nails were black from cleaning out the gutters.

'Huh,' he'd said. The back of his neck all red.

'What's it mean?' Mrs Wigg said, from by the stove.

His son looked up. 'It means, Mum, that she's going to take us to court if we don't sell the farm and give her half the money.'

Mr Wigg had to put both palms on the table he felt so unsteady. 'Why is she doing this?'

Mrs Wigg frowned. 'My sister and I didn't get anything out of the farm. It was for our brother; we understood that.'

Their son rubbed at his face. 'You married into a farm, though. That's what was expected,' he said. 'Times have changed.'

'I'll call her,' Mr Wigg had said. 'Try to talk her round.'

'I think it's a bit late for that, Dad.'

Mrs Wigg had sighed, made her lips thin. Once that look would have pulled both children into line, but not anymore. 'This is no way to settle family matters.'

Their son had looked at his hands. 'She wants half. She tried to say this six months ago. We didn't listen.'

Mrs Wigg's throat was flushed. Her voice shrill. 'She's not entitled to half. She hasn't even been here, let alone worked the place.'

Mr Wigg put his hand on hers and looked to his son. 'What do you think we should do?'

'What she wants us to. Sell the farm and give her half after expenses. Instead of the deposit. It would cost a whole lot more to fight it in court, and there's no guarantee we'd win. Better the money stays in the family than goes to a pack of lawyers.'

It had seemed like a lot of huff and bluff to him, but their son knew how these things worked better than they did.

His wife had convinced herself that their daughter-in-law had driven the decision to give in, it suiting her to move further away. Truth be told, Mrs Wigg had probably not helped matters by always popping in and trying to influence his son's wife, or by speaking as if they still had a say in how the farm was run. Young folk wanted to get on with their own lives, and that was hard to do with your parents always looking on. It might have made the decision to sell a bit easier, but Mr Wigg didn't see that his son had had much choice.

And so it was that the place was put on the market. All those years, all that work, had come to nothing: dust in the wind.

# Leaves

**M**r Wigg used half-blows over the edge of the anvil to shape the piece of round quarter-inch into a shoulder: the leaf's stem. He heated it again and hammered it into a gentle taper towards the tip, a bit like a tiny arrowhead. This time he tried to work in some movement, hammering it into a soft curve.

He heated the tapered section, taking care not to burn the fine tip, and flattened it out on the face of the anvil until it was as thin as he dared and peach-leaf shaped. Next, he gently heated the leaf and worked the vein down the middle with a chisel, going deeper this time, to get more of a fold. He heated the stem and hot cut it to length with the hardy, then hammered it to follow the leaf's curve. Finally, he quenched it in the water bucket and fished it out with his fingers.

He smiled. A bit rough but a peach leaf nonetheless. He placed it on the bench next to the earlier attempts: its more primitive forebears. He flicked through his sketches again, leaving a black smudge on each page. He figured he needed one hundred and fifty more; he'd need to get a bit quicker or never finish the thing.

He sat on the bench outside the workshop to eat an orange in the sun, punching his thumb through its thick skin and pulling back the peel. A fine spray of oil misted across the back of his hand. There had been no frost this morning, and they were past the equinox, so perhaps the worst of winter was gone. He ate the orange, segment by segment, until it was gone. He'd had better crops, much sweeter fruit a few years back, but today, eating an orange from a seedling he had planted thirty years ago tasted as good as anything.

The Orchard Queen would have had plenty of oranges, acres and acres of them, to keep her soldiers healthy. Her palace gates would have been adorned with curling metal grapevines, the walkways covered with a wrought-iron pear arbour. The walls of the main hall would have featured a persimmon in autumn as well as the usual tapestries, and the forecourt of the palace built around a sculptured peach orchard, mirroring the real one below. In times of peace, the team of blacksmiths would be employed crafting artworks for the queen and gifts for royal visitors. The queen's crest, a stylised version of the peach grove adorning the green banners flying from the castle walls, would be stamped on every piece.

Mr Wigg rinsed his hands under the tap and dried them on the towel by the workshop door.

By lunchtime he had another four leaves, each similar enough to the others but with individual texture and markings. Hammering the vein was the hardest part, keeping the chisel steady for several hits a leaf to get a continuous line. There were bound to be days he wouldn't be able to do it well enough. And time was marching on. He needed a team of smiths with steady hands.

# Chilling Hours

Mr Wigg forked chook manure into the ground beneath the persimmons. They said nothing, not wanting to draw attention to their bare limbs and the smell of rotting poo at their feet. It was good for them though, and they knew it: an investment in the future.

Except for the citrus, all the other fruit trees were bare, too, ghosted limbs in the still foggy morning. Their energy was now focussed inside, gathering the vigour to bud in spring. Any chat was short and grumpy. The trees' chilling hours were like the hibernation of the bear: better left uninterrupted.

The Traubners were laying out irrigation pipes, running all across the place in a grid from the bore. Mr Wigg's son had come out to resolve some problems with the pump and ended up replacing the thing, which was not before time.

Mr Wigg laid the fork and shovel in the wheelbarrow and stopped to rub at his arm, aching again, and puffed. It was winter, without a hint of the heat that bothered him sometimes. He should be able to handle a bit of shovelling; when a man can't even fertilise his own fruit trees he ought to give up. He leaned for a moment on the barrow until the feeling passed. He had not eaten much breakfast this morning, only toast, perhaps he just needed something to eat.

He took his time fetching the hose to water in the manure, whistling as he went. The sun was directly above him as he wheeled the barrow back to the workshop.

Mrs Wigg had always finished her fertilising first, as she had shorter distances to travel. She had her secrets, too, as to what went in the mix. He suspected a little of his nitrogen went missing sometimes, and even some chook feed as well as the usual chook poo, taking it from the ladies at both ends, so to speak. Whatever the ingredients, her roses' blooms spoke for themselves.

Every good gardener held a few things back, even from their husband or wife. It made for a better show to produce fruit and flowers, as if by magic, than to detail all the hard work you put in. There was a certain amount of information – experience gleaned over the years – you would happily share, among friends, but there were always a few little tricks or superstitions best kept between you and your garden.

Mr Wigg could smell burning wool. A log had rolled out of the fireplace and off the edge of the hearth. He put his soup bowl down and pushed himself out of the chair. He slid the log back with the poker, smoke biting at his eyes. The tongs wouldn't grip well enough to pick it up, he had to flip one end onto the fire and then the other, making a great mess of coals and sparks. He coughed and leaned the poker against the fireplace. There was an ugly scorch mark on the carpet, which his son would be sure to notice next time.

Mr Wigg set himself back up with his bowl and soup spoon and frowned at the television screen. All the controversy surrounding the Springboks all-white South African rugby tour of Australia had come to a head in Brisbane, where things were so out of control that Premier Joh Bjelke-Petersen had declared a state of emergency. They had moved the match from Ballymore to the Exhibition Stadium, where they could better fence the ground to keep out protesters, and the police were fronting off with angry crowds, arresting hundreds.

This apartheid business was no good at all, but to his mind, politics had no place in sport. Not in this country. It wasn't as if it was the players' fault.

He couldn't help wondering if all the fuss was to distract from the fact that South Africa had won the Test, leading the series two–nil. None of it boded well for South Africa's scheduled cricket tour over the coming summer.

# The Queen's
# Smith

'That sure is a lot of eggs, Poppy.' They were piled up in two large ice-cream containers on the kitchen table.

'The ladies have been laying their heads off,' Mr Wigg said. 'So I thought we'd make meringues with the whites and custard with the yolks.'

'Yay!' Fiona said. 'Grandma used to like making custard.'

Mr Wigg stopped. 'You can remember that?'

Fiona nodded. 'She showed me how to eat it with a very, very small spoon so it lasts longer.'

Lachlan started getting out bowls and whisks and wooden spoons.

Mr Wigg blew his nose and cleared his throat. 'Mr Traubner was telling me that in France, when they are making the wine in the summer, they use a whole lot of egg whites. So they give all the yolks to the baker and he makes special little custardy cakes, called canelés.'

Fiona sat up on the stool. 'Can we make those?'

'Maybe next time. I'll have to ask Traubner if he has a recipe.'

'Are there really egg whites in wine?' Lachlan said.

'They use them to make the wine clear. I'm not sure how it works. But I don't think the eggs actually stay in there when the wine gets bottled,' he said. 'How about you be in charge of the custard, Fiona? Lachlan can deal with the meringues and I'll help both of you.'

They nodded together, as if of one mind.

Lachlan started ferrying eggs over to the bench. 'Do you have any more cricket stories?'

'I want to hear more about the Peach King,' Fiona said.

'Well, I do have a little story about the Orchard Queen's blacksmith,' he said. 'Why don't I separate the eggs and deal them out? Yellows for Fiona, whites for Lachlan.'

They leaned back from their bowls and counted the eggs in, commenting on relative size and colour.

'The queen's blacksmith strode from anvil to anvil, his hands clasped behind his back. His apprentices hammered and tapped and quenched. They were to complete a hundred new shields for the queen's army by morning. To be presented to this season's fresh young recruits at the queen's birthday parade.

'The smith paused to offer a few words of encouragement here, a helping hand there. After all, he had been the queen's blacksmith for over fifty years. What he didn't know about smithing, wasn't worth knowing.

'They worked underground, so as not to disturb the queen with their hammering. The caves were deep and dark but warm in winter with all the forge fires burning. People said it was easy to tell a smith apart; he had big hands and shoulders, and a pale face that rarely saw the sun. Like dwarves, they said, when being unkind.

'The queen's blacksmith moved on to another cave, where the senior smiths were completing the decorative work on finished shields. Can you guess what the Orchard Queen's soldiers wore on their shields?'

'An orchard?' Fiona said. She had already splashed yolk on her shirt and her nose.

'That's right. And how would you draw an orchard?'

Lachlan frowned. 'Maybe just a few trees?'

'Yes,' Mr Wigg said. 'Five trunks and one top, a kind of collective canopy. Peach trees, of course.'

'*Obviously*,' Fiona said.

'The queen's blacksmith pulled a special vial from the inside pocket of his leather waistcoat. A secret concoction he had wrangled from the dwarves up in the hills after several long nights of drinking and playing cards. He added a few drops to each of the silver peach tree groves when they were all hot and molten. Then he bent to breathe over them as they cooled, whispering the old secret words:

*Deflect steel and arrow,*
*Keep fear from marrow,*

*And bring all the Orchard Queen's men home.'*

Lachlan and Fiona had stopped beating.

'Keep going. You need stiff peaks, Lachey. And we want the yolk folk good and creamy for the custard.'

Mr Wigg threw another piece of wood on the stove. 'The queen's blacksmith spent a bit longer with the one-armed smith, Billy. He was working on the captains' shields, which had a peach-coloured diamond embedded in the tree crown. Billy had been the most promising of all the apprentices through the years and the queen's blacksmith had thought he would hand everything over to him one day. But one winter, they were working through the night, and the pile of big oak barrels they were hooping got loose. Billy tried to stop them getting away but one of the barrels crushed his arm against the wall.'

Fiona stopped.

'Now we're just going to add a secret ingredient to our meringues,' Mr Wigg said. He took a little glass bottle of rosewater from his pocket, and counted out ten drops.

Fiona giggled.

'Just whisk that in a little, Lachlan,' he said.

Fiona was on the way to the stove with the custard, wooden spoon at the ready. 'Billy's arm?'

'Oh, yes. His arm was crushed and useless. The queen's doctor said it could not be repaired. They had to remove it to save his life,' Mr Wigg said.

'With a saw?' Lachlan said.

Fiona shut her eyes and put her hands over her ears.

'You're done, Lachey. Now plop one spoonful at a time

onto the trays. That's it,' Mr Wigg said. 'Of course, everyone thought that would be it for Billy: no more smithing. But when he was well again, the queen's blacksmith convinced him to come back to work. He learned to do everything one-handed – although it was all a bit slower – and could still tackle jobs only the queen's blacksmith himself could do better.

'After all of the others had gone home, the queen's blacksmith returned to his own anvil. He fired up the forge and set out his tools, singing all the while. The fire burned white. He bent to remove the queen's birthday gift from its hiding spot behind a stone in the wall.

'The silver bracelet was a peach tree branch, that would creep up around the queen's forearm. As it was to be a surprise, he had to enlist the help of the queen's tailor to match her measurements. The bracelet changed with the seasons, beginning as a bare branch in winter, budding and shooting in spring, fruiting in summer, and finally, its leaves taking on all the shades of autumn before beginning again. Only he didn't have it quite right yet; it kept sending out spikes in late winter, like the thorns of a rose. For obvious reasons, that would not do at all. And there were only a few hours till dawn.'

'The custard's ready, Poppy.'

'Good, just pull it off to cool.'

Lachlan carried a tray of messy meringues in front of him. 'Can someone open the oven for me?'

Fiona bowed. 'Yes, your Majesty.'

# Wood

Mr Wigg gathered up his dirty work clothes from the bathroom floor and headed for the laundry, carrying the pile out in front of him like a back-to-front tortoise. He felt for the half-step down onto the verandah, shuffled out in his slippers and fell full-length onto the cold boards. *That mongrel cord.* The washing provided a soft landing for his upper body but he had banged his ankle on the door frame. He sat up. Sniffed back tears. A purple egg was growing and his dry skin had split open; blood running down into his slipper. He lifted himself up in the doorway, gathered the clothes together again and threw them in the machine.

He limped back into the bathroom, glaring at the cord as he stepped over it. There didn't seem to be any Dettol, so he just placed a square bandaid over the spot. 'Right,' he said. It was time to get young Scott back out.

Mr Wigg fetched his glasses from the kitchen and sat on the stool near the phone, the cold creeping through his slippers. He tucked his feet up onto the stool's footrest and flicked through the teledex. Scott wasn't there, but he left a message with Scott's wife.

His daughter's number was on the same page, underneath a series of old ones his wife had crossed out. She and his wife had spoken once a week until all the trouble. Not for long – his daughter never seemed to have too much to say – but enough to stay in touch and get a sense of what was going on with one another.

Mr Wigg dialled the area code, hesitated, and put the receiver back on the cradle. He needed to think about what to say. There was no point going in half-cocked and blowing it. Maybe he could ask her to come down for Christmas, but he should speak to his son first.

Mr Wigg winced as he pulled his boot over his ankle. It was more sore than a little scrape should be. Perhaps he was getting soft. 'I know, I know, it's my own fault.'

He limped behind the wheelbarrow, cursing the distance to the woodpile. It was no longer a pile but a scattering; he was down to the very last already. He collected it all, even bits of stringybark that had come away from the wood. He should tell his son he needed another load but he would be busy putting the crop in. Last winter had been the time, too, when he started on about moving into town. The chainsaw had gotten hard to start and his son had taken it away to 'fix' it. In the end, he didn't bring it back, saying it was too dangerous and too much work for a man his age.

That was his independence gone, right there. If you had a chainsaw you could always keep yourself warm with fallen branches and dead wood. Off the side of the road if you had to.

His son had left him the axe, though, which was just as dangerous. When Mr Wigg had still been at school, the Lander twins used to play a game to amuse themselves while chopping wood for their family of nine. They would take turns placing their hand on the chopping block while the other brought down the axe, seeing who would be the first to baulk. As they got older, and teenage hormones surged, they grew bolder and bolder, leaving it until the last second to pull their hand away, or chopping the axe into the block just a few inches from the splayed fingers. Mr Wigg had declined to participate on several occasions, though some of the other boys had had a go and survived. Mr Wigg's father had always said work tools were not for playing with and that seemed like sensible advice.

Mr Wigg couldn't remember now which twin was swinging and which one laid out their still-growing pink fingers, but one winter one twin brought the axe down right on target and the other didn't move his hand; they had each called the other's bluff. One lost all the fingers on his right hand, and the other had to take him to hospital on the back of a horse because the only vehicle was out and their parents weren't home. Poor bloke had to learn to write with the other hand, and struggled to keep up with his brother on the farm.

Mr Wigg wheeled the barrow over to the old yellow box behind the chook yard and gathered up a few thick sticks and a fallen branch. He pushed his load back to the workshop door, his ankle still paining against his boot.

He dragged the branch inside, lifted it up on the workbench and started the circular saw. Its blade spun, sped up, and disappeared into a whir. He cut the branch into three lengths; enough to keep the lounge room warm for the evening.

# Rosehip

Once the property went on the market, and people in town started talking about it, his wife had faded away. She could not have beaten the cancer but, looking back, he could remember the moment she gave up fighting.

After the sale to the O'Briens fell through, the agent had held an open house, and for two hours that afternoon cars had slowed down on the road to turn in, parking along the drive. Many of them just came for a look, the equivalent of kicking the tyres. His wife had watched from the front verandah, pale and thin-mouthed. She had put on a gardening shirt, taken her secateurs and gone out to the roses, which he had thought a good sign, but when he went to fetch her for lunch, he found she had beheaded every rose. He had stood there blinking at the carnage before gathering up as many as he could and arranging them in vases and bowls about the house, which she then pretended not to notice.

He caught her, in the following weeks, watching their son's house from a chair on the front verandah through the binoculars. She would report, over Saturday lunch, if someone had come to look. 'They're from Victoria,' she'd say, or 'there was a flash car', and 'all the coming and going is stopping me sleeping.'

There wasn't that much traffic, or the place would have sold sooner. It wasn't the potential buyers that interrupted her sleep but pain, and they both knew it. He had resorted, in the end, to hiding the binoculars, though he didn't feel good about it, and eventually she gave up looking for them.

The following year, the roses had produced an unusually high number of hips – and not through any special care from him – as if defecting to the fruit side of production.

During the Second World War, when fresh fruit was in short supply in Britain, rosehips had been used in jams and desserts, the local children sent out to raid the hedgerows. His mother had occasionally made a rosehip syrup up at the old farm, harvesting the more established bushes to keep up their vitamin C levels, probably during lean times, though they had remained largely unaware of any outside events until they were young men.

Rosehips, he had read, could also relieve rheumatoid arthritis, which seemed ironic, since his wife had handled them, with increasingly arthritic hands, most of her life.

Mr Wigg fetched another rosebush from the back of Traubner's ute. Young Traubner was already half way down the hill, digging the holes ahead of them at the end of each row. It was a bit strange at first, planting roses in ground where wheat had grown, and before the grapevines even went in. But it was certainly more enjoyable than sowing crop.

Roses were susceptible to the same diseases as grapes, Traubner said, mildew and the like. They were an early warning system, signalling when treatment was needed. And they would look nice.

It would have been difficult for Mrs Wigg, but he liked to think that even she would have got excited by a truckload of rose bushes. There were only a few different varieties, picked for their hardiness rather than colour and bloom, but the paddocks were starting to look different.

Traubner had the irrigation system working, and was filling the holes with water a few rows ahead, giving it time to drain away. Mr Wigg pulled free the packaging from his rose and waited while Traubner flicked in a shovel full of cow manure, then two shovelfuls of loose soil. Mr Wigg spread the rose's roots out over the mound.

'Let's fill her up then, eh?' Traubner said, shovelling soil to fill the hole.

Mr Wigg patted down the soil, scooping away a hollow, and making sure the graft union would sit at least three inches above the ground.

'I hear your wife had a gift for roses?'

'Sure did. One of the finest collections around for a time.' Mr Wigg brought back two roses this time, to save a trip. He could've done with a sit down but he figured they'd stop for morning tea soon. He was looking forward to another one of the little cakes Mrs Traubner had made with the almonds he gave them.

'I reckon we're getting the hang of this,' Traubner said. 'Get it done in a few days.'

Just as well for the roses, it wasn't good for bare-rooted stock to lay around for too long. 'Tough starting everything again like this?'

Traubner shook his head. 'I like this part. And this time it's all ours. No brothers or fathers to fight with.'

Mr Wigg smiled. 'I know what you mean, there.'

Traubner watered in the last rosebush for the section.

Mr Wigg straightened his back. 'Long while till you get any return though.'

'It is. We'll start making wine this vintage, though. With some of my brother's grapes.'

Andy threw the shovel on the back of the ute. 'Thought you old blokes would have caught up to me by now. Too busy talking.'

'There's an art to planting a rose properly,' Mr Wigg said.

'Beginning with a perfectly dug hole,' Andy said.

Traubner shook his head. 'Why don't you set up morning tea for us then, since you're so efficient?'

# Rhubarb

**M**r Wigg planted out new rhubarb crowns. They really should have gone in a few weeks earlier, their little roots were already starting out of their punnets and into the world. The more established plants, almost ready to harvest, muttered among themselves in an unfriendly manner.

He patted down the soil around the last crown. The Romans had given rhubarb the name *rhabarbarum*, meaning barbarian, a tribute to the behaviour of the Siberians who grew it on the banks of the Volga River. Rhubarb's speech was crude, and muted by soil. Whether it was their barbarian heritage or their poisonous leaves behind their lack of manners, Mr Wigg wasn't sure, but the old were not at all gracious with the young.

Mr Wigg felt a little ungracious himself. England had won again, beating Pakistan one—nil in their Test series. At home mind you, but they had already taken over half the world once; it didn't seem right that they keep on doing it.

In medieval Europe, rhubarb had been more expensive than saffron and even opium, regarded rather differently, no doubt, than the second rate vegetable it had become these days.

Stewed rhubarb with custard had been Mrs Wigg's favourite winter dessert. It had been one of the last meals she had eaten – eaten and enjoyed, anyway – that winter.

'That,' she had said, 'was the best custard and rhubarb for years.'

Mr Wigg had looked up, surprised. His custard had turned out well, but truth be told, the rhubarb had been a little woody.

'Thank you for taking care of me,' she said. 'You've been wonderful.'

He had reached for her hand, cried at the thinness of her wrist, once so strong.

'It's all right, love,' she said.

Mr Wigg heard his son's truck roar past the house. He put on his parka and beanie, slid on his boots and tried to walk without limping out to the woodpile. His breath fogged in front of him.

'How long have you been out?' his son said.

'Used the last of it this morning,' Mr Wigg said. He'd had to scavenge wood scraps from the bin in the workshop to light the stove.

'Should have told me,' he said. 'Can't have you freezing to death out here on your own.'

'I knew you'd be here today.'

'You use it up faster than we do,' his son said. 'With the stove.' He leapt up onto the back of the truck and began throwing off bits of wood.

Mr Wigg took pieces from the edge of the tray and flung them off onto what was again becoming a heap. 'I could help you get it you know, make it easier.'

'It's all right, I just get a bit more when I do ours.'

Mr Wigg moved to the other side of the truck. 'How's that chainsaw going?'

His son grinned. 'Good. Still a bitch to start, though.'

The wood pieces were a mixture of ironbark and yellow box, trees long dead by the look of it. Half cut long for the fireplace, the other half short blocks for the stove. 'Should burn well, this lot.'

His son nodded. 'I've been doing some cleaning up before summer.' He stood to stretch his back. 'You thought any more about moving into town? Checked out any of those places?'

Mr Wigg reached for the last piece of wood, a knobbly bit of burl. He grunted with the weight of it. The latest batch of pamphlets had gone straight from the back step to the stove, disappearing in strange-coloured flames. 'No.'

'What does that mean? No, I haven't thought about it or no, I'm not going to.'

'Either way,' Mr Wigg said. 'You can do what you like when I'm gone. Until then, I'm stopping right here.'

His son pressed his lips together. Made them thin, like his mother. 'We worry about you.'

'I manage all right,' he said. 'I can call. And the Traubners aren't far away.'

His son sighed. 'What's happening with Andy?'

Mr Wigg leaned on the truck bed. 'He didn't qualify for any of the exemptions. And he passed his medical. So I guess he has to go.'

His son shook his head. 'Unless he fails his security clearance. Turns out to have reds under the bed.'

Mr Wigg snorted. 'Don't think so.'

'It's funny if you think about it,' he said. 'We locked up all the Germans around here in the last war and now we want their sons to fight for us. Well, for the Yanks.'

Mr Wigg didn't think it was funny at all. Blokes they'd called friends and neighbours disappeared for months just because their name was Schultz or Pfeifer.

'Henrick going to be able to manage on his own?'

'His wife's pretty capable,' Mr Wigg said. 'And I'm going to give him a hand with the planting.'

His son swung down off the truck. Clapped him on the shoulder. 'Is that right? You get to be the vigneron after all, huh?' he said. 'Hang on, got something for you.' He reached into the truck cabin. 'It's the paperwork for the patent. You just have to fill it in, enclose a copy of the design and send it off. The pictures we took are in the envelope already.'

Mr Wigg took the papers. 'Thank you,' he said.

'Have you thought of a name?' his son said. 'The kids want you to call it Mr Wigg's Fabulous Drying Machine.'

Mr Wigg smiled. 'That's not bad, actually.'

Mr Wigg piled wood on the fire and sat down with his tea, lamington, and *The Orchards of the World*. His lamingtons were a bit rough, not neat and fine like his wife used to make. He'd probably used too much icing. Young Scott was coming tomorrow morning and this time he meant to offer the boy a cup of tea for his trouble.

Mr Wigg had been right through his book, several times now, but kept coming back to the section on southern France, with its fenceless vineyards stretching across the hills and walled orchards: damp with green secrets. The towns were walled, too, built into impossible hillsides and burnt orange in the late afternoon light. Every spare bit of space was used: blackberries crept along the sides of roads, apples wept over culverts and bridges. Fig trees tumbled over stone walls. Truffles grew beneath walnut trees on the mountainsides.

The tree-lined canal – man-made it said, running right across the country – had been used to transport wine up to Paris in the old days. By the time it arrived, half had gone missing: stolen or drunk along the way. The boatmen thought nothing of sharing the vintage with friends or those showing them hospitality on the journey, and the transport company did not accept any responsibility. He kept meaning to tell Traubner – who complained about the drivers trucking his wine up from down south – that story. They always seemed to lose or break a case or two, as if they had encountered rough seas.

There was a complex system for moving water from the river around the town and out to the gardens and orchards, a miniature canal along the roadside. Mr Wigg could not tell exactly how it worked from the pictures; he would have liked a diagram, and details on how the flow was controlled.

There was even a village baths, and a fountain, surrounded by plane trees. He wouldn't mind living in a town like that, with its gardens and markets. Old folk out strolling in the evenings and looking out for each other. Still with a place in the community. The little rooms up at that home in town were a far cry from that, with their sterile walls and bland food. Few visitors. And not a garden in sight. Blokes only went there to die and everyone knew it.

# Wires

Young Scott already had the new wires hanging out of the hole in the wall beneath the dryer. He finished his mouthful of dried apricot. 'So, how does this contraption of yours work?'

'Just warm dry air, really,' Mr Wigg said. 'Lots of ventilation. Fan makes it a bit quicker.'

Scott nodded, hooked the wires up to the power point cover. 'Impressive.'

'How's your wife?'

'Good,' he said. 'She said to thank you for the peaches; she loved them. We both did. Actually . . .' he paused, screwdriver hovering. It couldn't be a good thing for an electrician's hands to shake that much. 'We're going to have a baby soon.'

The magic of peach crumble perhaps. 'Well, congratulations,' Mr Wigg said.

Scott had gone all red up the throat. 'Thanks. Bit earlier than we planned but, you know . . .' He screwed down the power point cover and plugged in the drying machine. Its fan whirred between them. 'There you go.'

'That's great,' Mr Wigg said. 'Just great.'

'Better than tripping over that cord all the time,' Scott said.

Mr Wigg nodded. Rubbed his sore ankle with a socked toe. 'The manhole's in the hallway?'

'That's right.' Mr Wigg had half been hoping Scott would forget about his old wiring. The whole lot probably needed replacing and who knew what it would cost.

Scott unplugged his drill from the laundry, packed it up. 'Okay. Let's have a look up there, then.' He carried his ladder in and set it up. Took a torch from his tool box. 'At least any snakes will be asleep this time of year.'

Mr Wigg watched him move aside the manhole cover and disappear into the ceiling. He stood on his footstool to reach a jar of brandied apricots, and another of poached pears; you never knew what a woman would feel like eating when she was expecting. Mrs Wigg had liked pears and golden syrup with their daughter, ham and tomato on toast with their son. And custard right throughout both pregnancies.

Mr Wigg pushed the stool back out of the way and carried the jars to the kitchen table. He stoked up the stove and dragged the kettle over the heat.

He could hear Scott moving about above him. It had probably been twenty years since he had been up there himself. When they put in the new insulation. He never had been fond of tight spaces and it had been a rotten itchy job.

Mr Wigg watched Scott's foot appear, then another. The rest of him followed.

'It's not too bad up there,' he said. 'I'd recommend replacing the wiring over the lounge room and bedroom sooner rather than later. It's all on one circuit and looks like a bit of water got in there at some stage. But nothing too urgent.'

Mr Wigg smiled.

'I'll do you up a quote and you just tell me when you're ready.'

'Sounds good. Got time for a cuppa while you write it up?' Mr Wigg said. 'Warm up a bit.'

Scott looked down from the ladder. 'Sure, Mr Wigg. That'd be nice.'

# Vines

This time the Traubners had pre-dug the holes, which had the planting moving along much more quickly. Still, all the bending and shovelling of dirt back in over the vines' roots was work enough. Mr Wigg had offered to take a shovel – to do his fair share – but they had waved him away, working better as a father and son team. Once he could not have imagined not being able to hold his own with other men. He was having to get used to it now.

The holes were about six feet apart and bigger than they had dug for the roses. They were starting with the cabernet. The rows were wider for them, Traubner said, to allow for more sun and greater air circulation. The rain had made their work easier and freshened up the grass now growing between the rows. It apparently kept the soil together, and looked pleasing at this time of year.

Handling the cabernet vines was a treat. Their lineage ran back to French vines several hundred years before. It had made Mr Wigg a bit nervous at first, worried about damaging them with his clumsy hands. It was not unlike planting any other fruit tree, but the scale of the project, planting en masse and according to a plan, had him feeling as if he were a part of something larger.

It reminded him of fencing with his brothers, though he would rather plant vines than posts. It was something he had missed, working with other blokes. He and his brothers, for all their fooling around, had got through the work in no time. Each working day went by without him noticing.

Young Andy flew ahead, his body and energy levels without limits. He went back and forth from the ute, fetching vines and laying them out by their homes-to-be, moved the ute along when he got a few rows ahead, and filled in his holes like a mad thing. Mr Wigg thought perhaps the young fellow could afford to take a little more care settling the vines into the soil, but Traubner said nothing. The two of them didn't talk too much but they seemed easy enough with each other. Andy having to go off to war had put things in perspective no doubt.

Traubner started talking up the qualities of cabernet, and the different flavours finding their way into the wine. Mr Wigg could imagine cedar and berry, and wood from the barrels, but the idea of a grape tasting like mint was beyond him. It had to be said, however, that his olfactory capacities were decidedly on the wane. Just the other day he found a dead mouse in the trap in the pantry, which had been there for days. He soon smelled it up close, but once he would have picked up the first whiff from the hallway. Or heard the trap snap, for that matter.

Mr Wigg lowered in another vine, taking a moment to spread out its roots before Traubner began shovelling in the dark soil.

Andy delivered another lot of vines, still trussed up like captured prisoners. 'He's not still going on about bloody cabernet? Let me guess, the king of grapes.'

Mr Wigg smiled. 'What's your favourite then?'

'I like the riesling,' he said. 'It's honest. Reflects the flavour of the soil it grows in. I'm looking forward to tasting what we've got here.'

'Andy's the traditionalist in the family,' Traubner said. Riesling's big at home. And he has some sort of *affinity*: can pick the region of almost any riesling from a blind tasting.'

'Sounds like an old man's talent,' Mr Wigg said.

Traubner and Andy laughed, working all the while.

Mrs Traubner came down for lunch, setting up a picnic out in the sun between the rows. The ground had dried off with the sun and light breeze. She laid out cold meats and cheese and a loaf of freshly baked bread. Mr Wigg fetched the cider he had brought today from the esky. They drank from little glasses with thick green swirling stems.

'What do you think of wine growing, then, Mr Wigg?'

Mr Wigg smiled. 'It's like planting a giant orchard,' he said. 'Takes real vision. A long-term view.'

Mrs Traubner looked pleased at that. Offered him some more pickles.

'You use dill in these?'

She nodded. 'I can give you some if you like them.'

'That would be lovely,' he said. 'What about your family? Are they winemakers, too?'

'They are. From the opposite side of the Barossa. We met at a wine show, waiting around for our parents.'

Andy groaned and stuffed bread and ham into his mouth. A story he had heard a few times before, no doubt.

'A double dose of wine in your blood, then,' Mr Wigg said.

Andy nodded. 'Too bad if I wanted to be a vet.'

'Blood tends to flow its own way,' Mr Wigg said. 'A bit like your riesling.'

Andy looked away, towards the mountains. Slid his hat back on.

Mr Wigg sipped his cider, propped up on one elbow. The bubbles tickled the whiskers in his nose. He yawned and stretched; he could do with a nap but he didn't figure that was part of the Traubners' routine.

Mr Wigg's back stiffened up after lunch, which Traubner was kind enough to notice. He was switched to watering duty, keeping the seedlings on the truck damp and watering the vines in as they went, which gave him a bit more time to look around. Cars slowed as they passed along the road, having a good stickybeak, no doubt.

His hands were cold from the water but the sun was warm and there were signs of spring, too: a hint of warmth on the breeze, and blue wrens hopping along on the wires, as if they'd been installed for their benefit.

They were filling in the gaps between the roses, the fruit between the thorns, and the grapes were beginning to dominate. The place was starting to look like a vineyard. There was something about the way the lines followed the slope and contour of the land that reminded him of the lands of the Orchard Queen. Of course she would have had a few more labourers at her disposal and had them work a little faster.

'When you're ready, Mr Wigg.'

'Sorry.' He twisted the nozzle and adjusted the flow with his thumb. He was getting quite good at the process even if he did drift off now and then.

'Got a date yet?'

Andy shook his head. 'Still waiting.'

Mr Wigg nodded. 'Every day here's a bonus. Days like this, anyway.'

Andy looked back over what they had planted. 'That's for sure.'

# Vein

Mr Wigg parked his ute in the shed, leaving the engine running while he listened to the end of the news. India had beaten England in a Test match *in England* for the first time in history, taking the series and ending the English winning streak at last. 'Ha!' The Poms might have given the colonies cricket, but now the colonies were taking it back.

He gathered up his mail and struggled out the door. It had been a while since he could say every muscle was aching, but it was. What muscles he had left, anyway. He placed the letters on top of his grocery box, and lifted it from the ute's tray. The cold breeze had his bones all clumsy and brittle and he swore when he jarred his finger on the side rail.

He carried the box inside, resting it on the fence to manoeuvre through the front gate, and followed the path around to the back door. He'd only done a few hours' planting up at the Traubner's today, to finish the cabernet, then come back via the mailbox, but the persimmons and eggs he had left out were gone, and the gutter finally repaired.

Mr Wigg put the box down on the step and walked back to the workshop rubbing his right arm and chest. It wasn't as if the box was heavy, or carrying it was as hard as the work he did every day. Certainly not as hard as the last week or so.

He'd noticed a parcel on the workshop bench wrapped in butcher's paper; perhaps his son had left some scissors or knives for sharpening.

Mr Wigg cut the string and pulled the paper away. It was a veining chisel. Antique but in good condition. It had been sharpened, any rust cleaned off. *Where the hell did he get hold of that?* Mr Wigg measured it against one of his leaves. It was perfect. The curved blade allowed for making straight lines without lifting the tool. 'Just rock and hit, rock and hit,' Smithy used to say. He would be able to work faster, and get a neater line.

He hurried inside to put the groceries away, the smell of fresh bread tempting him to an early lunch. He stoked up the stove, pushed in as much wood as he could fit and slid the pot of soup onto the heat. Even when he used the end of his stump now it didn't hurt. Though it gave a funny tingle sometimes, as if it was still trying to get a message through to the missing tip.

The mail held nothing of interest: a few bills, something from the government about travelling on the train for free.

He stuck that on the calendar; perhaps it could be an excuse to visit his daughter, see his grandchildren again.

The local paper talked up the rugby team's prospects for making the finals for the tenth year in a row and announced plans for a village green, which would mean cutting off one end of the main street and planting shade trees, lawn and a garden. Mr Wigg spread the paper out on the kitchen table and reached for his glasses. The businesses down that end of town weren't going to like it, except maybe the café, but most of it was wasted space at the moment, a desert-like nature strip and too much bitumen. Mr Wigg traced the lines of the story with his finger. The project was the result of a bequest from old Verna Cartwright and her friend Nan Young, who both died last winter. The Arts Council had chipped in, too, sponsoring a state-wide sculpture competition to find the green's centrepiece. 'Huh.'

The soup was boiling. He cut two slices of bread, buttered them and placed them on a plate, ladled soup into a bowl, moved the pot off to the side, and carried his meal over to the table. Closing date for the sculpture competition was the end of November, only three months away.

# Spring

# Swage

Spring was well-sprung by the time Mr Wigg had made enough leaves. The orchard was in blossom, the birds nesting, and bees buzzing in the wisteria outside. His workshop floor was covered with half-assembled branches, the bench with piles of iron leaves.

He had taken advantage of a couple of quiet days while Traubner waited for the chardonnay vines to arrive, and when his tremor had seemed to disappear, to tackle the base. It had still been a struggle, forge welding the heavier pieces and trying to get the twisted look he was after. He was happy with the peach tree's feet though, gnarly twisted roots that had taken on a life of their own. The craft shop had rung wanting some more pokers, too, but he'd told them he couldn't get to it for a few weeks. He didn't feel he needed to say why at his age and he'd just look a fool talking about the competition, so he left Mrs Webb's disappointed silence hanging where she left it.

All that remained to make was the fruit. As his wife liked to remind him, he did sometimes have a habit of leaving the hardest things till last. Mr Wigg scribbled out his design and started again. They had to be three-dimensional to look right but couldn't be solid, or they'd be too heavy and impossible to forge. Casting was an option but fiddly. He'd have to make one to work off, then a mould, then melt iron or steel. Bronze would be nice, and a good colour, but that was hardly realistic. For a proper artist, maybe. The sort of hip young thing from a Sydney art school who would actually win the prize.

Mr Wigg's original plan had been to make two halves and forge-weld them together but he didn't really have the tools, or the skills, for all those curves. His wife would have probably had an idea. She would pretend not to notice or understand his scribblings, but when he hit a problem, she usually had a suggestion or two.

The books referred to a swage block. The traditional ones were huge, almost a second anvil, with a world full of depressions and holes. Smithy had had one, but must have hauled it away with him, like Atlas, when he left.

There was a crate full of tools from the shed up at the old farm somewhere, perhaps there would be something he could use in there.

The machinery shed doors were heavy and stiff; built big in the days when he could not imagine growing old and frail.

He pressed the light switch and waited for the fluorescent tubes to flicker on. Jagged piles gathered dust around the walls. Things he had thought too valuable to throw out, or that could be of use someday, and then left too long. The box was under some sheets of unused roofing iron but he dragged it out, stamping on a few red-back spiders. Miserable things, always lurking in the dark.

Oil stains marked the spot where the old header used to be parked, and then his son's newer machine before he bought the other farm. There was something about the smell of dust and oil together, of farm sheds, that always made him feel like a boy again, playing in the old machinery with his brothers before they were old enough to see them as instruments of work.

Mr Wigg cleared away cobwebs with a stick and rummaged through the crate. He pulled out a solid block with a smooth hollow at its centre. 'Ha!' It was a deep concave swage, used to make ladles and the like. Smithy had turned those out by the dozen on Saturdays, to sell for a little extra money. Now Mr Wigg saw it, he could picture how the peach might work.

He turned off the shed lights and pushed the doors closed, struggling at first to line them up so he could slide the latch across. The swage was cool against his belly, even through his shirt. Heavy, too, for its size. Mr Wigg puffed his way back to the workshop door and rattled it open one-handed.

He threw more wood on the fire and pumped the bellows until he had a critical mass of red coals. He heated a square of sheet metal, placed it over the hollow and hammered it out against the curve. It took a few goes, and he knew he had weakened the metal a little too much, but he soon had a half sphere. He repeated the process to form its twin, tapping a split down the middle with a chisel to form the fruit's bottom.

He sat them together on top of the anvil and lined them up. The two halves didn't fit together. Not even close. A forge weld wouldn't work; he'd have to use the oxy.

Mr Wigg wheeled the tanks over to the bench and set himself up. He worked with filler and blue flame to try to get as fine a bead on the join as possible but his hands shook. When he had finished, the join was bumpy and the globe still too symmetrical to be mistaken for a peach.

He tried reheating the fruit and shaping it, punching a depression in the top, thinning it toward the bottom, but the final product was a bit of a mess. Like an over-ripe peach squashed in the bottom of a bucket.

The light was nearly gone outside and cold air was sneaking in under the door. He had spent the entire day making a mottled silver and black peach that was nowhere near good enough. Any blacksmith offering such a poisonous looking object to the Orchard Queen would have his head pruned at the neck.

Mr Wigg tidied up, struggled into his red parka and beanie and hurried out to feed the chooks. He left the peach sitting on the bench.

# Blossom

**M**r Wigg wandered through his arbour of blossom. The apricots, dressed in white, and the nectarines and peaches in rose pink, reached for each other with fresh generosity. Their foliage was a rich emerald, the air heavy with perfume and the hum of bees.

Confucius, it was said, had taught his students in a wood of apricot trees. In China, too, apricot meant 'educational circle'. It must have been difficult for the young scholars – in the prime of their lives – to concentrate in the heady surrounds of spring. Their thoughts likely wandered, at times, to more physical pleasures.

Mr Wigg checked the centre of a few peach flowers to make sure they were fully formed, taking care not to stir up any bees. According to the Peach King, it was the gypsies who spread the peach throughout Asia and Europe, while the original peach tree was praised and petted behind the walls of the queen's orchard. The queen's gardener had spent years experimenting with grafting, developing his magical techniques to produce more trees, unaware the horse had already bolted.

The history books told it a bit differently; peaches were first cultivated in China, gradually making their way into India and Persia, before Alexander the Great conquered the Persians and brought all their best foods and spices to Europe.

Perhaps the Peach King's story was a lost chapter of the tree's European history. After all, trees without provenance were often disregarded, and gypsies tended to be blamed for more than they could possibly be responsible for. It was all too convenient to make scapegoats of a roaming group of people who could just be moved on.

His mother had not been sure of the original peach cultivars in the orchard back at the old farm. While Jack – who had selected and planted them before Mr Wigg was born – probably knew, he left them unlabelled and the knowledge died with him. Mr Wigg still remembered the bite of those peaches, likely an ancestor of the more hardy Anzac they replaced them with after the First World War.

Mr Wigg had finished school by then, and was working the farm. His mother had given over management of the orchard after supervising his first efforts with the pruning shears. She had smiled and wiped her hands on her white apron as if her job was done. If only he had found it as easy to let his own children go their own way.

Modern peaches tended to live fast and die young, their production dropping off after fifteen or so years. It was harsh, but there was no place in an orchard for a tree unable to bear fruit. The peaches and nectarines blooming around him were Mr Wigg's third generation, while the apricots, pears and quinces had been here as long as he had.

It was difficult for the apricots and other old originals – as Mr Wigg understood all too well – seeing the new trees come and go, growing so rapidly, with barely the time to acquire any wisdom at all.

Someone was knocking on the front door. Mr Wigg pulled himself up off the couch, his book tumbling to the floor; he must have fallen asleep. He wobbled along the hallway, lightheaded. The sun outside was bright.

'Afternoon, Mr Wigg.'

Mr Wigg blinked. The young fellow stood on the front verandah in his new uniform, all ironed and stiff. 'You're off, then?'

'Just came to say goodbye. And to thank you for the trees. I got them planted out all right.'

Mr Wigg nodded. 'I'll keep an eye on them if you like.'

'When I get back, I want to talk to you about the perry. Dad and I think it could be a goer,' he said. 'We've set aside an area for the pears and we can make it in the off-season. And I haven't forgotten about the smithing lesson. I want to make a candelabra for the dining table. Surprise Mum.'

Mr Wigg smiled. 'Sounds good.'

'All right, then,' he said. 'I'd better get going. Dad's waiting.' Mr Traubner was sitting in the ute, looking straight ahead.

'Keep your head down over there, son,' Mr Wigg said. 'And I'll see you when you get back.'

They shook hands. Young Traubner hesitated, then turned on his shiny heels and walked down the steps.

# Copper

It was a couple of days before Mr Wigg got back into the workshop. The tree was always on his mind, but the vegetable beds had needed weeding and it was time to plant the carrots. He had decided to put in more tomatoes this year so he could start making his relish again and the new beds needed working over. The days were warming up, getting longer, but there never seemed to be enough hours.

His peach was not where he had left it. It was sitting on the other side of the bench, near the window. Had it rolled itself over into the sun? Or was it trying to get closer to its tree? Perhaps it would roll off and attach itself to the tree overnight, which would be handy, because he hadn't figured that part out yet.

Now that he knew what he was doing, his next peach was finished in half the time and looked twice as good. But it still wasn't good enough. The metal was difficult to shape properly and the weld too shiny. Not to mention the colour was all wrong; people would probably think it a rotten apple, something made by a witch or wicked stepmother to poison a beautiful princess.

Mr Wigg frowned. There was a rumbling outside, like a passing train. Or as if something large were being rolled up the front path. It wasn't the day for his son to drop in; perhaps it was Traubner with a barrel. Or even an empty half-barrel for planting herbs. He wouldn't mind that at all.

Mr Wigg wiped his hands and stepped out into the day. The air was still and heavy with pollen. Dragonflies flitted about the birdbaths. It was his son after all, pushing a copper water tank in front of him with his boot.

'Got something for you,' he said. 'I had to replace the old system at our place.'

Mr Wigg blinked.

'It's for your peaches,' he said. 'I saw what you're up to in there.'

Mr Wigg stared at the metal, orangey and shining in the sun. And soft. Compared to sheet metal anyway. 'Now why didn't I think of that?'

'It must have taken you hours.'

Mr Wigg nodded. 'A whole day,' he said. 'I just made another. Come and see.'

His son followed him in, dragging the tank.

Mr Wigg held out his new peach.

'Pretty good.'

'Only took half the day this time,' Mr Wigg said. 'But the copper will be a lot easier,' he said. 'Thank you.'

'Have you shown any of it to the kids yet?'

'I was going to wait until it's all together.' It had been tempting to show them some of the leaves; he had done a good job on them. Although they loved to watch him at the forge, he found it difficult to hammer and watch two sets of little hands in the workshop; there were just too many possibilities for accident. And he was looking forward to seeing their faces when they saw the finished tree.

His son nodded. 'They'll be impressed.' He put the peach down next to its mate. Scuffed his boot on a crack in the concrete. 'We're finally set up at the new place. Settled. We were wondering if you'd like to come over on Sunday. For Father's Day lunch.'

'Sunday?' Mr Wigg cleared his throat. 'I'd like that very much.'

'Good. I'll pick you up around eleven?'

# Tradition

**M**r Wigg set his place at the kitchen table for lunch. The last of the vines had gone in late yesterday and the job that had seemed to stretch out forever at the start, was done. Mrs Traubner had given him a couple of jars of pickle, which he was enjoying, though not as much as he had after a hard morning's work. The trouble with having company for a while was that you missed it all the more when it was gone.

He heard the washing machine shake itself to a stop. His shirts finally done. He would wear his best one to his son's tomorrow, though it would probably only make him more nervous.

When they were first married, Mr Wigg had liked to make a bit of a fuss about Sunday lunch, and give Mrs Wigg a break from the cooking. He would roast a piece of meat, no matter the weather, and a whole lot of vegetables. They would eat in the dining room, with all of the good cutlery and china and a glass of wine. He would put a record on, and his apron, and get busy right after morning tea.

Usually he would do a dessert as well, a pudding or a pie instead of their usual stewed fruit and custard. Afterwards they would play a game and lounge around, bellies content.

Years later, Mrs Wigg admitted it hadn't been the gift he had imagined; the mess he made caused her more stress than doing the cooking herself. That had pulled him up right there, shown how wrong-headed you could be about things if you didn't pay attention. After that, they took turns at cooking on Sunday and whoever cooked had to clean up, which was fine with him. And they didn't have roasts in summer, because Mrs Wigg didn't care for the heat it generated or the flies it brought in.

When their son and daughter came along the Sunday lunch became a more pedestrian affair, a matter of finding something everyone would eat; any meal without squabbles was a good one. They always tried to have the afternoon off to spend time together as a family, even if it was just watching a movie on television beside the air conditioner.

He and his wife had both got it wrong after their son was married, trying to persist with tradition by inviting the newlyweds for lunch every Sunday. He and Mrs Wigg had taken their time, as they had become used to being on their own, only serving dessert up around three.

Mr Wigg should probably have noticed his son getting irritated, especially when his tremor started to get worse, having him clanging his plate and bowl with his cutlery halfway into the afternoon. His son was, of course, keen to get back out to work, not believing in the Sabbath or days of rest. They were still finishing their house, and working on their garden, and time with him and Mrs Wigg was time away from their own life. His daughter-in-law's parents often came out for Sunday dinner, too, so it didn't leave them much time to themselves.

It became a monthly occasion instead, and he and his wife, without any discussion, drifted back to the traditions of their first years together, sometimes even ending up back in the bedroom, which was a pleasant surprise for both of them.

# Lunch

His son's new place, 'Connondale', was right out the other side of town and towards the mountains. As it turned out, the property had once been owned by a distant relative of Mrs Wigg's family, the Wrights, which was something. That was before the Thompsons, who farmed the place for two generations until their only son was killed in a silo accident. It was hard to imagine how a father could ever forgive himself for that. Word was they had moved up to the coast somewhere to get away from all the sadness.

Tragedy had kept the price down. They had hoped for someone out of town, who didn't know the whole story, but it hadn't worked out that way. Truth be told, every property had its history, its ghosts, good and bad.

The gums along the gravel road were bigger than he remembered, casting a pleasant shade. The farm itself was pretty, stands of ironbarks sweeping down from the hilltops and a string of willow-lined dams by the drive. His son slowed down to cross the ramp and Mr Wigg smiled to see the mailbox he had made them shining from the top of a post.

Someone had planted river oaks along the entrance, only a year or two ago from the looks of them. The breeze sang in their branches and they waved their arms in time. An eddy swirled in to lift red soil from the driveway.

Lachlan and Fiona came running down the porch steps, wild hair flying behind them. 'Poppy, Poppy!'

His son opened the car door, shielding Mr Wigg from the children's force until he had got himself up and steady. They hugged his legs and looked up at him, grinning.

'Hello, mischiefs,' Mr Wigg said, a hand on each head.

'We got you a cool present,' Fiona said.

'Shhhh,' Lachlan said.

They walked either side of him up to the front door, slowing their pace to his. His son carried the oranges and lemons Mr Wigg had brought from home. Mr Wigg stopped to take off his boots and stepped into the dark hallway.

His daughter-in-law, pink-cheeked from the stove and smelling of roast spring lamb and rosemary, ducked out to give him a kiss before disappearing back into the kitchen.

'Would you like a beer, Dad?'

'That would be good, thanks.'

The children led him into the lounge room. Picture windows framed a boulder-strewn valley, with a good cover of spring grass. It was decent cattle country up here, while the lower paddocks, catching the silt spill from the creek, were good for cropping. They had less land to work with than back home, which would be tough, especially with a mortgage. His son had said his wife was working a few days at the stock and station agent to help out, now the children were both in school.

Out the other way, beyond the clothesline, Mr Wigg could see they had fenced off an area for an orchard, and put in a dozen or so trees.

'We helped plant them,' Fiona said.

Lachlan rolled his eyes. '*I* helped. Fiona was too busy saving worms from the kookaburra.'

Fiona frowned. 'There's apples, and apricots, and oranges, and lemons, and peaches, of course!' Fiona counted them off on her tiny fingers.

'Don't forget quince,' Lachlan said. 'We still had that one in a pot from the old place.'

Mr Wigg smiled. 'Quince? Well, that's a bit old-fashioned, isn't it?'

Lachlan and Fiona shrugged.

'I wanted to put in persimmons, too,' said his son, stepping through the sliding door with the beers. 'But I couldn't get any.'

His son had, at least, inherited an appreciation for persimmons, trying his hand at persimmon bread and persimmon pudding. Mr Wigg took a mouthful of beer to try to wash down the lump in his throat.

'Your mum has some drinks for you two in the kitchen,' his son said. 'And she needs you to help set the table.'

'Old Bill Spies can order persimmons in,' Mr Wigg said.

'Yeah?' his son said. 'Want to have a look at what we've done so far?'

He followed his son out the side door, concentrating on not spilling his beer. The sun was hot on his head and his hat was hanging in the hall.

Mr Wigg stopped at each tree, checked its progress. 'Well.' The soil was a bit high on some of the trunks but they'd done a good job over all. His son must have been paying more attention over the years than he thought.

'We could do with a bit of help with the orchard.'

'You know what you're doing,' he said. 'Soil looks pretty good here. Might get a bit dry in summer though.'

'There's a decent dam down the back and a pump on it already. We want to put in a dripper system before Christmas.'

Mr Wigg nodded. 'They'll need it until they get established.' He and Mrs Wigg had ferried water around in buckets their first summer. Every tree had survived though, despite a week of hot winds, and they had built up arms like wrestlers.

His son stopped in front of a young white peach. Coughed. 'Would you consider coming to live with us next year, Dad? There's a granny flat out the back,' he said. 'Grandpa flat, I guess.' He looked at his boots. 'Needs a bit of work, but we could do it up pretty nice. The kids would love to see more of you, and there'd be a new orchard needing your touch.'

Mr Wigg sipped his beer, licked a bit of foam from his lip. The trees were too young, the orchard too new. He'd never see them bear fruit. 'I appreciate the offer. But I wouldn't want to leave my own place,' he said. 'And I'm managing all right at the moment.'

His son opened his mouth to say something but shut it again.

'Be nice to stay overnight sometimes, though. Save you driving me home.'

Fiona ran out in bare feet, her lips bright orange with soft drink. 'Lunch is ready!'

They ate at a long table in the dining room, looking out over the courtyard lined with lavender and rosemary. Mr Wigg examined the white bowl in front of him. A handful of mayonnaisey yabby tails nested in a green pear-shaped boat.

'We caught the crayfish this morning,' Lachlan said.

His daughter-in-law smiled. 'I told them it was still too early, but they came home with half a bucket full. The avocados are from my sister's place. On the north coast.'

'Avocado,' Mr Wigg said. According to one of his fruit books, avocado was an Aztec word meaning testicle, named for its shape and its reputation as the fertility fruit. He scooped up a little of the smooth flesh with the splade and squashed it against the roof of his mouth. 'Well.' He mixed the next scoop with a yabby. 'This,' he said, 'is delicious.'

His daughter-in-law smiled. 'I used your lemons in the mayonnaise.'

'You've been busy in the garden, I see,' Mr Wigg said.

She nodded. 'We wanted to get as much as we could established before summer.'

Fiona put down her splade. 'Mummy, I don't think I like avocado.'

Mr Wigg winked and raised his eyebrows.

Fiona giggled and slid her bowl over.

Mr Wigg was still mopping up gravy with his potatoes. His son fidgeted at the other end of the table and Mr Wigg tried not to let his knife touch the plate. His tremor was getting the better of him, wanting to ring everything like a bell.

Lachlan and Fiona were kicking each other under the table.

'All right, you two. Bring it in,' their mother said. She cleared the table, picking up stray peas from around Fiona's plate.

The children came back carrying an oddly shaped parcel and put it on the table next to him. 'Happy Father's Day, Poppy.'

Mr Wigg felt himself getting all choked up again but managed to give them a hug. He opened the card and read it aloud. Sat it up above his placemat. 'Now then.' He ripped the wrapping away with an exaggerated movement, revealing a new hat. 'Just what I needed,' he said. 'That's going to be handy coming into summer,' he said. 'Thank you.'

'There's more,' Lachlan said.

Fiona hopped up and down. 'The clues are in the picture!'

Mr Wigg lifted the hat and squinted at the page. Predominantly green and white. 'Well,' he said. 'There's a cricket match going on here.'

'We're *going* to the cricket!' Lachlan said. 'You, me and Dad.'

Mr Wigg smiled. 'Really?'

'The third Test against the South Africans, in Sydney. 'I'll drive us all up,' his son said. 'We've booked a hotel. Thought we'd make a bit of a weekend of it.'

'Why can't I go?' Fiona said. 'I like crickets, too.'

Lachlan groaned.

'We're all going to Sydney, poppet. But you and I will go to the zoo,' his daughter-in-law said. 'To see the elephants.'

❧

Mr Wigg carried his plate and glass out to the kitchen. 'That was a lovely meal, Margaret. Thank you.'

She smiled. 'You're welcome. I'm glad you enjoyed it.'

'You've got the place looking real nice, too. I hear it was all a bit run-down.'

'Just left empty too long. The kids have been a big help cleaning up,' she said. 'Especially in the kitchen. You've done a great job with them.'

'I have the time,' he said. 'It's much harder with your own. Coming at the busiest time of your life.'

'That's true.' She ran hot water for the dishes, squeezed in yellow detergent.

Mr Wigg looked around for a tea towel, found one hanging on the rail of the stove door.

'You don't have to do that,' she said. 'Would you like James to show you around the farm?'

'He's been talked into playing Monopoly with the children,' he said. 'Besides, I like to get used to a kitchen first.'

'Best thing about the house,' she said. 'Though I miss the stove at home.'

He picked up a wet plate with his left hand, making sure he kept a firm grip on it. 'You can see the orchard from the window there, that's nice.'

# Beetroot

**M**r Wigg planted corky beetroot seeds out next to the silverbeet. They were, after all, of the same species, *beta vulgaris*, native to the European seashore. Over the centuries they had grown apart: one bred for its leaves, one for its root. Both took their name rather to heart, swearing and cursing at any slugs or snails approaching, even sparrows perching nearby. A little more politeness and the birds would attend to the predators for them, and have a tidy lunch, but old habits die hard.

If there was one thing he had learned it was that raging against everything was a waste of energy. There was a balance to things that tended to sort itself out over time; you were better off flowing with the tide.

This year he was going to try Chioggia, as well as the usual globe beets. The so-called Queen of the Beetroot World had been grown outside Venice since 1583. She was super sweet with alternating red and white concentric rings. Mr Wigg gave her the run of the outer edge of the bed, expecting her to lord it over – or lady it over – the plainer globes.

He cleaned up and put his tools away. The spring air was heavy and sweet. He walked a circuit of the garden, praising azaleas, daphnes, and the rhododendrons. The beds of violets were rich and damp, the jonquils all out en masse. With the exception of her roses – exhibiting a fuller palate – his wife had favoured purple and white flowers. It wasn't as showy as some gardens but together with all the green foliage, it had a gentle uniformity.

The rose garden was still rather splendid, despite his neglect. His wife had tended to them several days a week, running the show with a firm hand. Mr Wigg preferred to let them go a little wild. It wouldn't do for competition, or the long term, but their showing days were over and his innings well into its twilight.

It didn't pay to think about what would happen to the garden once he was gone, or the manner of his dismissal. Leaving a ball only to have it knock down your stumps would have to be the worst way to get out, followed closely by knocking the ball onto your own stumps. And leg before wicket was always something of an anti-climax. Caught was probably his preference, perhaps off a big shot into the outfield; at least you went while having a go.

Mr Wigg carried his dinner in on a tray to eat in front of the news. He had half caught something on the radio earlier about the South African cricket tour.

He sliced through a pork chop, cut it into square bites. Dipped a piece in last year's beetroot relish. The Australian Cricket Board was in crisis talks with the (white) South African Cricket Board. They showed footage of ACB Chair, Don Bradman, boarding a plane, and protesters vowing 'non-violent direct action', whatever that was supposed to mean.

The South African Cricket Board had included two black players in its touring team, Abed and Williams – in an effort to appease world opinion – but the South African Government had vetoed their selection. As it turned out, Abed and Williams had declined the invitation anyway, but the whole thing had the cricket world in a furore.

Bradman was off to try to sort it out. He had been at the Rugby Test in Sydney with the South African Ambassador, so had seen first hand the security issues the cricket tour would face. Yet he insisted plans would go ahead, and that politics had no place in sport. The South African cricketers themselves, he argued, were opposed to racism and had 'tried harder than our protesters to do something about it'.

Bradman was a sour-faced fellow, for all his success, but he spoke sense. If anyone could make the tour happen it was him. Mr Wigg hoped so, anyway; he wouldn't get too many more chances to go to Sydney, or see a live international match. Three generations of Wiggs on the white picket fence, that would be something.

# Among Vines

**M**r Wigg worked his way along the row next to Traubner. He figured Traubner was going slow on purpose, or maybe he was just more thorough. They were pruning the vines back to three buds, which seemed a bit severe. It wouldn't be until next year that they would be trained onto the wires. It was enjoyable work though, and Traubner good company. He was more chatty without the young fellow around.

The furrows were still weed free and willie wagtails chattered around them, flicking their tails this way and that, as if with old friends. Water from the bore dripped all along the rows. Beyond the vines, the paddocks were as green as he could remember seeing them for years.

They stopped mid-morning for smoko, sitting in the shade of the ute. Traubner produced a thermos of tea and some ham and mustard sandwiches on fresh white bread.

'Your family have any vines back in France?' Traubner said, mouth full.

'My grandmother's family apparently had a reasonable parcel of land,' Mr Wigg said. 'And grew grapes. In Languedoc, I'm told.'

Traubner grinned. 'I'd believe it. You're a natural.'

Mr Wigg smiled. 'Not sure if their wine was any good. I haven't found anything about it in any of my books.'

'I like the wines from that area. Interesting soil. They make a good earthy Mourvèdre. Carignan and Cinsault. They're all underrated in my view.'

'What about you? Whereabouts in Germany was your family?'

'They're still there. Some of them, anyway,' he said. 'On the Rhine, where it meets the Moselle. It's called *Das Deutches Eck* – the German Corner – near a town called Koblenz. They grow grapes on the banks of the river.' He moved his arm in an arc to indicate the steepness of it.

Mr Wigg nodded. 'There's a picture of the Moselle Valley in a book I have. The vineyards are very neat. And built a bit like terraces.'

'That's it,' he said. 'All very German.' He pulled a stiff, serious face.

Mr Wigg laughed. 'Funny to think how we ended up here, instead of speaking French and German,' he said. 'Of course, you probably *do* speak German?'

'A little.' Traubner poured Mr Wigg another mug of tea. 'It is funny to think about. I've spent time there, learning the traditional ways of winemaking from a great great uncle or some such. And I feel at home, there's a certain settling of the blood. In the village. On the land. I could easily stop there but it would be such a different way of life, you know?'

Mr Wigg nodded and sipped his tea. It was difficult for him to imagine living anywhere else now but he would have liked to have seen some of those villages and orchards in Europe for himself. Taken Mrs Wigg to see his family's chalky hills lined with vines. Though, as it turned out, the vines had come to him. 'Have you heard from Andy?'

'He got through his training. Said it was worse than digging holes for me,' Traubner said. 'So he's off in a few days.'

'I keep hoping it will all be over before he gets there.'

'Me too,' Traubner said. 'You miss working with your son?'

Mr Wigg coughed up a bit of sandwich that had gone down the wrong way. 'Working with him not so much. But I always thought he'd be right here.'

Traubner refilled Mr Wigg's mug with steaming tea. 'I'm real sorry it didn't turn out like that,' he said. 'But sometimes a little distance can be a good thing.'

# Sugar and Sap

The trees' leaves were green and lush, thick with their rapid spring growth, and the peaches' pink blossoms were coming to an end. The younger trees – the peaches and nectarines – were particularly silly at this time of year, all full of sugar and sap, and giggly with the tickle of bees and the pollination process. The older and wiser trees – the apricots, apples, persimmons and pears – were getting impatient with their noise.

Mr Wigg laughed. It would be nice to be young again, though somehow retain your wisdom. 'Come on now.'

The pears had always been sensitive during spring, as they were not self-fertile, like the others, but required cross-pollination. 'It's no laughing matter,' Bon Chrétien muttered. Bickering like a long-married couple most of the year, the pears began dipping their branches at each other in early September. Beurré Bosc recited sonnets in that particular tone and Bon Chrétien responded with made up songs about the qualities of pear blossom.

The apples enjoyed a bit of cross-pollination, too. Although not strictly necessary, it produced higher fruit yields. Perhaps as a result, they were rather less bashful, singing love songs non-stop for all to hear.

The pears and apples were at the absolute mercy of the other trees during this time. The persimmons led the refrain about false sentimentality and stooping to animal-like behaviour.

His books didn't have much to say on the sexuality of fruit trees. Mr Wigg figured it was best to keep quiet until the storm of pollen had settled. Or to keep them off subject with his own nonsense rhymes.

*There was an Old Man of Girgenti,*
*Who lived in profusion and plenty;*
*He lay on two chairs,*
*and ate thousands of pears,*
*That susceptible Man of Girgenti.*

Mr Wigg had met his wife at a dance up at the old farm. Their families knew each other, though not well. She had kept on at school a while after he left. Blokes were always asking her to dance – she was a fine-looking woman – and she mostly said yes, just for one dance, but Mr Wigg had hung back.

He'd been hanging back a little too long. Most of his friends were married, or engaged at least. His brothers, too. When it came about that he was on his home turf, as it were, for the Summer Ball, he figured it was his best chance. He had lashed out and bought a new shirt and tie, spent time polishing his shoes. The week beforehand was one of the longest of his life. If his mother noticed his sudden interest in decorating the hall, or installing lights throughout the garden, she said nothing. The night before he had barely slept, and was not looking his best. But when his wife-to-be – not that he dared think that way right then – arrived, she looked straight at him and smiled.

They danced a couple of times during the night, and chattered a bit. She had laughed at his jokes and seemed interested in what he said about fruit trees.

'I love to garden,' she'd said. 'But we don't have much of an orchard at home.'

Later in the evening, he had fetched her a drink, his mother's punch, and asked her if she would like to take a tour of the gardens. He couldn't hear her answer at first, for the sound of his own blood rushing about his ears, but she was smiling. 'It's all lit up,' he said. 'For the dance.'

'I'd like that,' she said.

There was a bright moon that night, too, the gods shining on him for once. There were other couples sitting on benches outside the ballroom, holding hands and talking softly to each other. He'd felt his neck flush hot.

'My sister and I played in a tennis tournament up here last summer,' she said. 'But I didn't see you.'

Had she been looking for him? 'I think we were selling stock that day,' he said.

'Your mother is a very good player.'

'She is,' Mr Wigg said. 'Used to compete when she was younger.'

'Can you play?'

'I can hit the ball back,' he said. 'But it's not pretty to watch.' She laughed.

'I hear you and your sister are hard to beat.'

'At doubles,' she said. 'Singularly we are less remarkable.' She took his hand to step down into the sunken garden. 'We practised together our whole childhood. I know exactly what she is going to do and vice versa.'

'Is that right?'

'On the court, that is,' she said. 'The rest of her life is a mystery to me.'

Mr Wigg smiled. Her younger sister, Mabel, was to marry the new bank manager. A funny looking bloke. 'You'll miss her at home.'

She looked up at him. 'Yes and no. A bit more quiet will be welcome.'

Mr Wigg sipped his punch and pointed out the different irises, massed around a fountain. Lanterns swung shadows on the grass. 'The lawn is underplanted with crocuses and jonquils here; it looks lovely in spring.'

They had strolled back through the orchard, strung with coloured globes, each surrounded by a halo of insects. He had shown her the young peaches, their fruit already set, but it was the old apricots she admired. She had stood between them, chin tilted up at the stars. 'I read that there is a Turkish saying about apricots, something like, "It doesn't get any better that an apricot in Damascus".'

Somehow he'd had the courage to reach for her hand. She had turned and kissed him, before he had time to think or fumble. It was a kiss sweet with fruit and summer and youth, and he had known, right there, that she was his future.

# Old Rivers

**M**r Wigg put his radio in the wheelbarrow with his tools to keep him company while he picked peas. He tossed them into the ice-cream container, singing along to 'Old Rivers'. He and his wife had always argued over the words; she insisted Rivers wanted to walk among trees – rather than clouds – although she had never had much of an ear for lyrics. You would find both climbing a mountain, of course, but Mr Wigg got the sense the fellow imagined being part of the sky, rather than the earth he had spent so much time ploughing.

The sun was warm on the back of his shirt. It was time to do away with a singlet for working. He could hear everything growing and budding around him. A pair of blue wrens chattered about in the shrubs edging the rose garden, the male torn between pride in his own splendour and pursuit of the female.

When the container was full, he sat it in the shade and fetched his shovel and fork. He worked at turning over the other end of the bed, tossing out any weeds. The zucchini needed to go in, and a fresh lot of lettuce.

A kookaburra sat on the gutter, diving down to snatch any worms he unearthed. Mr Wigg straightened and tossed up a particularly fat one. The kookaburra swooped across, caught it mid-air, and settled on the fountain, whacking it on the edge as if it were a full-sized snake in need of killing and tenderising. Mr Wigg leaned on his shovel and turned up the radio to hear the midday news.

The South African cricket tour had been CANCELLED. Only seven weeks out from their first scheduled match. Bradman hadn't got anywhere, despite a long meeting with the South African Prime Minister himself. The Cricket Board had withdrawn its invitation for the team to tour, because of the South African Government's position on apartheid. 'We will not play them until they choose a team on a non-racist basis,' Bradman said.

Mr Wigg threw down his shovel and went inside for lunch. What a mess.

He shelled peas into a bowl by the sink. The technique he had spent fifty years developing was out the window with his missing fingertip. He needed his grandchildren around; they seemed to love the job, and their deft little fingers were better suited to it, although half the proceeds did tend to disappear into their pink mouths.

He and Mrs Wigg had trained their own children young, too, to pick and shell and peel. They had both been born in spring, two years apart. His first, and a son, had been a proud moment of course, but he had felt just as much joy when his daughter arrived.

They had talked about having another but, for whatever reason, it never happened. He had suggested seeing the doctor but his wife had said she was happy to let things be.

His wife had assumed their children would be close, as she had been with her sister. He had not assumed as much; he loved his brothers, and all that shared history and the land, bound them together, but they were each their own man. Had been since James was fifteen or so. That's just how it was.

His own children had struck out in different directions from the outset. His son could not wait to get into the world, the birth relatively quick for a first child. He did not grizzle and slept when he was put down.

His daughter took her time being born, gave everyone a scare. She had her little arm up near her face, which made the birth difficult. Turned out she knew what she was doing, protecting herself; if not for her arm, the umbilical cord would have gone around her neck and maybe done her some harm.

His son had said once, years later, that they had treated him differently, been harder on him. Mr Wigg had frowned and denied it at the time but all parents did tend to spoil a girl, and the youngest.

His son had seemed to want to work, and do everything as best he could, from early on. And it was true they had always expected he would take over the farm.

On his daughter's sixteenth birthday, Mrs Wigg had ordered in a fancy ice-cream cake from the city shaped like a pastel castle. He had seen the look on his son's face when he came in from milking the cows to discover the cake surrounded by presents. He realised, too late, they had not made a fuss of his son's sixteenth birthday at all.

His son had sung 'Happy Birthday' and eaten a slice, sat through all the unwrapping. He had made her an easel, for her painting, and fetched it from the workshop.

Mr Wigg had gone out to his son's room later, to talk to him, but he was gone.

# Wild Strawberries

The strawberries were coming on already, enjoying the warm days and regular overnight rain. Mr Wigg had revamped the scarecrow, marking out a fanged face and choosing one of his wife's more garish aqua dresses.

A picture in his *Orchards of the World* book, of woodland strawberries tumbling down over stone walls, had inspired him to plant some again. In Europe, they still grew along roadsides, in forests fringes and woodland clearings. If he had his time again, he'd build some stone walls in his orchard or around the edges; there was something so pleasing and substantial about them.

He'd grown his strawberries at the end of the usual beds, spilling out around the base of the tank stand. It was hardly a woodland but they were running comparatively wild. Woodland strawberries, like most wild food, were smaller but intensely flavoured. The children would enjoy picking them like gypsy children and he could tell them that *Fragaria vesca* have been eaten since the Stone Age; archaeologists had apparently discovered woodland strawberry seeds among the oldest human remains. Mr Wigg had found a recipe for strawberry tarts he thought the children would be able to manage, with his help. And he could tell their story to go with it.

First cultivated in ancient Persia, the strawberry's seeds travelled the Silk Road to the Far East and into Europe, where it was widely cultivated until the eighteenth century. Some of the village pictures in *Orchards of the World* suggested things hadn't changed too much since then. But in about 1740, French gardeners crossed *Fragaria virginiana* from eastern North America, which was known for its flavour, with *Fragaria chiloensis* from Chile and Argentina, which was noted for its large size, and the modern garden strawberry was born. The new always had its basis in the old, though it was soon forgotten.

The gypsies, expert in harvesting wild food, no doubt still knew where to find the old woodland strawberries that grew all over Europe. It wouldn't be a bad life, setting up on the banks of a stream by a tangled wood for a few weeks to forage strawberries or blackberries, and perhaps pinching the odd pheasant or rabbit for the pot.

His son had always taken great pleasure in stopping to gather 'free' fruit from the side of the road, which might otherwise go to waste. The figs he brought back from summer trips to a town an hour away – for reasons Mr Wigg suspected were not all that pressing – were better than any Mr Wigg had ever grown, black skinned and purple inside, probably a Black Genoa. There was a nectarine tree somewhere close by, on the way to the wheat silo perhaps, which produced small but lovely sweet fruit in random years without any assistance whatsoever.

Perhaps his son had a bit of gypsy blood in him somewhere, despite all that steadfastness. If not born the eldest (only) son of a farmer, he may have developed differently, more like those trees on the side of the road. Or the first peach tree out there alone in the wood.

Mr Wigg frowned down his neat rows and straight furrows. As hard as it was to contemplate, it was possible that his orchard didn't need him as much as he liked to think, and that the trees would go on producing fruit perfectly well on their own once he was gone.

Mr Wigg sliced dried persimmons crossways with a paring knife, adding them to the dried figs, sultanas, apricots, orange peel, peaches and pears already lolling around in the tub. He held a persimmon slice up to the light, admiring the star-sectioned pattern. Except for the currants, all of the fruit was his own. Even the peel. Not many could boast that of their Christmas cakes. Though, if he managed to get his fruit dryer out into people's homes that might change.

He poured two cups of Irish whiskey over the fruit and gave the tub a good shake. The smell was as complex as one of Traubner's fortified wines. He put the lid on the tub and carried it into the pantry. In a month's time, the fruit would be drunkenly moist and ready to use.

Christmas lunch was going to be at his son's house this year. Mr Wigg was to bring trifle as well as the Christmas cake, and, for the first time, would stay the night in the Poppy Flat, as the children had decided to call it.

He was also supposed to ring his daughter and ask them all to come. The answer would likely be no, but it was a father's job to try.

Sometimes he searched back through her childhood for a sign of the anger that came later. His son's character was evident from the start, though perhaps it had ended up worn a little sharp by his responsibilities. His daughter had had a capacity to shift to suit the occasion, which seemed a strength at first, but now he was not as sure. Perhaps they had never really known what she was thinking. Or what she wanted. It may have been that she didn't either.

There had been that look on her face though, when she didn't know he was watching, while she touched brush to page, and that seemed real. There had been a peace and calmness there that he had not seen since.

# Strawberry Tarts

Lachlan rubbed butter into flour.

'Now, Fiona. Can you measure out exactly a cup of cold water from the fridge?'

'Okay.' She climbed down from the stool, took the measuring cup he held out to her and ran to the fridge.

'Good. Now lightly beat the egg.'

Lachlan frowned over the bowl. Took the water from his sister.

'That's it. Now just roll it into a ball. It has to rest in the fridge for half an hour,' he said. 'Can you get me the baking paper, please, Fiona?'

Lachlan giggled. 'Does pastry get tired?'

'Yes, very tired from all that manhandling. It needs to cool down.'

Fiona pulled the drawer open with both hands, reached

in and held the roll of baking paper above her head like a winning baton.

Mr Wigg wrapped the pastry in one movement and handed it down to Fiona. 'To the fridge!'

'Do you have a story for us today, Poppy?' Lachlan said.

Mr Wigg nodded. 'I do. But let's get the custard done first,' he said. 'If you put the cream on, I'll beat the eggs and sugar. One clean bowl please, Fiona. And a wooden spoon for stirring.'

Fiona climbed up onto the stool, opened the cupboard and pulled out the blue bowl.

'Thank you,' Mr Wigg said. 'You can add half a teaspoon of vanilla to the cream, if you like. And stir till it comes to the boil.'

'Okay.'

Lachlan and Fiona bent their heads over the saucepan while Mr Wigg whisked.

'It's starting to boil,' Lachlan said.

'Good.' Mr Wigg poured in the egg mixture. 'Now take it off the heat a bit, and stir and stir until it starts getting thick,' he said. 'When it coats the back of the spoon, we'll take it off.'

'I love custard, Poppy,' Fiona said.

'Wait till you try it with the strawberries and pastry,' he said.

'Stir,' Lachlan said.

'I *am*,' said Fiona.

Mr Wigg stacked the dishes by the sink and wiped down the benches. 'How's the oven temperature?'

'About four hundred degrees,' Lachlan said.

'Good.'

'It's changing!' Fiona said.

'Okay. Slide it off the heat and keep stirring.' Mr Wigg looked over their little heads at the custard. 'That's it; make sure you're stirring right into the corners of the pan.'

'See if it coats the back of the spoon,' Lachlan said.

Fiona turned the spoon over and watched the custard drip off.

'That's it,' Mr Wigg said. 'Look out while I carry it over to the bench to cool.' He set the pan down on the breadboard and gave it another stir. 'Lachlan, you get the pastry.'

Lachlan ran out to the verandah and opened the fridge. 'Can we have a drink, please, Poppy?'

Mr Wigg nodded. 'Fiona, we need the cupcake tin, rolling pin and the scone cutter.'

Lachlan put the pastry on the bench and poured them all a lemon cordial.

'Now, Fiona is going to roll out the pastry, and you can cut the circles. And I have to make the orange glaze.'

'Okay,' Fiona said.

Lachlan gulped at his cordial. 'The story?'

Mr Wigg smiled. 'The queen's gardener grew very, very old. Mostly he supervised and taught his apprentices, and – with the queen's eventual, pouting agreement – promoted his best senior gardener to manage the day-to-day work.

'He still walked the orchard every day – even through the snow in the middle of winter – with a hand-carved walking stick the queen had presented him with on his eightieth birthday. In those days, eighty was quite a milestone, and some folk whispered that the gardener had used some of his magic to prolong his years. The stick was carved from pear wood, with a spray of fruit cascading down from its handle; it had a lovely spring to it.' Mr Wigg peered at the pastry. 'That's thin enough, I think,' he said.

'One day, the queen's gardener stopped by the outer orchard walls, to better hear a bird singing from one of the ancient pear trees. He thought he caught a flash of copper among the branches, as if a pheasant or a pigeon were perched there, but the song was unfamiliar.

'His walking stick quivered like a tuning fork. The queen's gardener wondered, for a moment, if the tree was calling it home.

'But then a woman climbed down, all dressed in autumn colours. Now who do you suppose it was?'

'His daughter!' Fiona and Lachlan said.

'That's right. And then a handsome boy jumped out, in a hooded green jacket.'

Lachlan smiled.

'And then a girl swung down from the branches like a pretty little monkey.'

Fiona giggled.

'"Father," his daughter said. "These are your grandchildren." And they hid in her skirts, their brown faces peering out. The boy was called Laslo and the girl Freya.' Mr Wigg greased the cupcake trays with the wrapping from the butter. 'That's the way. Cut them nice and close together so we get more.'

'The queen's gardener pulled silly faces at his grand-children. And then he straightened himself up and pulled a rainbow handkerchief from his deep pockets.' Mr Wigg reached into his own pocket and produced one of his wife's scarves, a swirl of colour. 'The queen's gardener squashed the handkerchief into his right fist like this.'

Lachlan and Fiona forgot the pastry and watched him poke the scarf in with his finger stump.

'And then . . . the hanky disappeared!' Mr Wigg flashed his empty palms. 'He reached out to little Freya . . .'

Fiona held her breath.

Mr Wigg put both hands up to Fiona's hair. 'And pulled the handkerchief out of her left ear!' Mr Wigg flashed the scarf in the air.

Lachlan and Fiona clapped.

'The queen's gardener's daughter embraced him and kissed his face. There was a little grey amongst the blonde around her temples now but he could see that she was happy and healthy, thriving out there in the woods like a wild peach.

'She produced a painted wooden box from her skirts and handed it to him. The queen's gardener held it for a moment before lifting the lid. There were two wooden trays, both divided into eight sections. Each compartment held a nest of seeds, and a tiny roll of parchment.

'"They are the seeds of all the best wild fruits I have eaten, Father. From lands to the north, where it snows and freezes white. From lands to the east, where the people ride wild horses and live in tents on the plains. From lands to the south, where the mountains are high, and the woodlands vast. And from lands to the west, where the oceans are warm, and fruit and flowers are always plentiful."

'The queen's gardener touched the seeds with a gnarled finger and gently uncurled one of the labels. The plant's name, in Latin: *Fragaria vesca*, along with scratchy growing instructions.'

Fiona frowned. 'What's Fragar vespa?'

'Well, the Woodland Strawberry!' Mr Wigg said. 'Speaking of which, you could start cutting off their bottoms.'

Fiona giggled.

Lachlan placed the last of the pastry rounds into the tins. 'Do we put them in the oven?'

'For fifteen minutes,' he said. 'Now, where were we?'

'His daughter gave him strawberry seeds.'

'That's right. And there were lots of other seeds, too. The gardener thanked his daughter. And he was very happy. But then trumpets announced the changing of the palace guard. "We must away," his daughter said. "Good bye, father." Laslo and Freya followed their mother up into the old pear tree. They looked back from the orchard wall, waved once, and were gone.

Mr Wigg took off his glasses to wipe his eyes. Fiona stood up on the stool to hug him around the neck. 'Make it have a happy ending, Poppy.'

Mr Wigg coughed and blew his nose on his wife's scarf. 'So, the queen's gardener planted the seeds and grew plums, loquats, blackberries, lychees, quince, persimmon, and . . . strawberries. What do you think the Orchard Queen said, when the old gardener brought her the first bowl of Woodland Strawberries?'

'Bring me more!' Lachlan and Fiona said.

'That's right. And luckily, this time, he had plenty more to bring her.

'And all the trees grew and grew and the Orchard Queen's magical fruit became famous all over the world. One day, on the eve of the gardener's hundredth birthday, some very clever men came to see the queen and with her nod of agreement – she was, by now, also very old, not to mention very round, with at least a dozen chins – began building a school for the study of plants. The first of its kind. And they named it after the queen's gardener. People wrote books about him and his orchard and studied his work, and he faded into legend.' Mr Wigg bowed. 'And that is the end of our story.'

Lachlan and Fiona clapped and grinned.

The oven timer went off. 'Okay, let's get them out and cooling.'

Mr Wigg set the trays on the cooling rack and cleared off some bench space for the assembly. 'Fiona, you can spoon the custard into the cases and Lachlan can arrange the strawberries. I'll put the glaze on top.'

When they finished, they had a platter of glistening wild strawberry tarts.

'Wow,' Fiona said, and popped the custard spoon in her mouth. Lachlan put the kettle on for tea.

Mr Wigg selected three of his wife's cup, saucer and plate sets from the sideboard and gave them a quick rinse and dry. They ate tarts with silver splades like royalty, their little fingers in the air.

Mr Wigg brushed pastry crumbs from his belly. 'What do you think?'

'Bring me more!' said Fiona.

Mr Wigg had made up the two beds in the sleep-out, his son's old room, for Lachlan and Fiona's sleepover. Cleaned up the room and aired it all day. What with tarts and dinner and board games, he was completely pooped. All that sugar up front had not been overly clever; Fiona had been in top gear all day, talking non-stop even while under the bath water, he was sure.

He checked his watch again; only ten minutes till bedtime. 'What do you think your mum and dad are doing tonight?' he said.

'Still painting, probably,' Lachlan said.

Mr Wigg nodded. That would be his son: to keep going until it's done. The granny flat wasn't large, but you needed plenty of time between the coats. 'And what colour did they decide on?'

'Well,' Fiona said, 'they *were* going to paint it aqua.'

'Were they now?'

'They were only joking, Fiona,' Lachlan said.

'I knew that.'

Lachlan poked her in the ribs, earning him a pinch on the arm. 'They settled on "Pear Shade".'

Mr Wigg smiled. 'Sounds nice. I could sleep in a pear shade, I reckon.'

Fiona somersaulted across the floor to kneel in front of *Orchards of the World*, open on the coffee table. 'Look, it's Poppy!'

Lachlan peered over her shoulder. 'That's not Poppy, stupid.'

She pouted. 'Looks like him. In the vegetable garden.'

Mr Wigg put on his glasses and leaned over, a hand on the back of their necks. 'That's a village garden in France; everyone has a plot and goes down each day to tend to it. And pick their tomatoes, like that fellow.' The old man did have a similar noseline. But surely he wasn't that round? Even these days. 'My grandmother was French,' he said. 'So you never know. Could be a distant relative.'

Fiona poked her tongue out at Lachlan.

'Why are the towns built like forts?' Lachlan said.

'That's a very good question. They did that to protect themselves against invaders. The Vandals and Visigoths, and then the Roman Catholic Church.'

Lachlan frowned. 'The church?'

The people in these towns had different beliefs. They were called Cathars. The big church didn't like that and declared war on them: a crusade.'

'That's not nice,' said Fiona.

'No. There was a particularly nasty fellow, Baron Simon de Montfort, who wiped out whole towns because they wouldn't give up their beliefs.'

'They built a fort to hide from Mont*fort*,' Lachlan said. 'That's funny.'

Mr Wigg smiled. 'There was another group, the Huguenots, who were extremely gifted plantsmen, driven out of France. Two hundred thousand of them.'

'Where did they all go?' Lachlan said.

'Holland, England, Germany, even South Africa,' he said. 'It's one of the ways plant knowledge spread around the world.'

'Is all this in the book?' Lachlan turned the page, as if looking for more exciting pictures of knights and torture devices.

Mr Wigg shook his head. 'I have some other books. The last bit I know, because my mother's ancestors were Huguenots, way back.'

'And they ran away to England.'

'That's right.'

'Look,' said Fiona. 'That lane is lined with poplars, just like yours.'

# Fox

He knew something was wrong when he woke late; the old rooster hadn't sounded his usual call. Everything was far too quiet. Despite the extra sleep, his body was slow to move. He wouldn't admit it to his son, but it took him a few days to recover from having the children stay over.

When he reached the chook yard, still in his pyjamas, he had to stop and lean on the gate. His ladies were lying about without their heads, in a sea of feathers, and the rooster was missing in action. What a waste.

The fox had dug right in under the fence and satisfied his sense of fun as much as hunger. The mostly eaten carcass of one of the ducks was discarded by the pond, the others gone without a trace. Someone's clutch of eggs was left untouched in the straw; a sad calm amid the chaos.

He had been meaning to fix the bit of fence that had

kicked up for weeks, but had been distracted by his tree. *Messing about in the workshop when there was real work to be done.*

Foxes had been a big problem early on. His daughter had been first at the scene on one occasion, and did not speak for a week. Luckily, there was no evidence left behind of her pet ducklings' fate, but even a five-year-old could figure out they had been a tender appetiser for a main fox-meal of chook.

In recent times, they had left the ladies alone. He hadn't even heard them yip-yipping for years. Though that could be due to his failing hearing rather than any decline in the fox population.

'Sneaky bloody fox!'

He couldn't stomach his breakfast. Just sipped a cup of weak tea. He would have to clean up yet, and repair the hole. Bury their sad little bodies somewhere that couldn't be dug up again.

He sniffed and his hand rattled the cup in its saucer. His poor ladies, he had really let them down. No longer fit to look after chooks! At least the children weren't here to see it; little Fiona would never forget it. Or forgive him.

When he had been a boy, he had seen animals slaughtered and carved up, and not thought too much of it. It had made him feel odd though, at the time, and it did occur to him, when he became more squeamish later in life, that perhaps it had done some damage. There were some things a child should be protected from for as long as possible. Reality came rushing along soon enough.

The first time a fox took Mrs Wigg's Hollywood ladies, she went off eating chicken for nearly a year. He had reinforced the fence and raised the ground around it. He didn't believe in trapping, that was just plain cruel. And he was quite fond of foxes, really. A flash of red by the side of the road, or out the corner of your eye at dusk, was somehow cheering. A bit of wildness still in the world. It wasn't their fault they had been introduced, after all.

He shot at any he saw around the place, though, to give them a bit of a fright. The time his daughter's ducklings had been the victims, he'd lost his temper and shot a fox dead, and they didn't come back for years. It hadn't sat well on his conscience though. Like a bad case of reflux, it kept coming back up. Refox, he'd called it, and packed his guns away.

You wouldn't talk to anyone down at the pub about those sorts of feelings, or over drinks after bowls. Farmers hated foxes and rabbits and roos, taking food from the table as they saw it; you had to have a hard heart. Young blokes, several sheets to the wind, liked to outdo each other with gruesome stories of shooting and unnecessary torture, which he couldn't abide, whether it was possums, pigs or feral cats. Every creature deserved some dignity the way he saw it. Another of his faults, he supposed, being too damn soft.

# Courting

Mrs Wigg had stopped playing tennis a few years after they were married. To be fair, it was initially because her sister (and playing partner) was pregnant, rather than anything he did, but Mr Wigg always worried about it. Neither sister went back to tennis after having children, which was true of many women around the district, but those two had been especially good, and he had imagined them playing socially, at least, till well into middle age. Everyone had been sorry to see them stop, especially when the regional trophy went to Canowindra. Then her sister moved away, her husband getting a position in a larger bank in the city, and it seemed there was no going back.

Mrs Wigg had said she didn't miss it too much, or her sister, but he had never been convinced. She had her garden, she said, and her family.

When he had started playing bowls, he had tried to kid her to take up tennis again for fun. 'It's a waste, you not playing,' he'd said. She gave him a look, and joked about legs of a certain age not being seen in a tennis skirt. He'd put his head down at that, because that was one of the reasons he had loved to watch her – him and half the district, no doubt – when they were courting.

Hindsight was never any use to anyone, except to torture themselves, but he probably should have tried harder. She had never really been the same after their daughter left home; the girl in her disappeared for good. Maybe picking up a racquet again would have brought her back.

It would have been good for the children to see that side of her, too: the flashing white magic of her on the court.

His parents had both given him advice leading up to his wedding. His father's was straightforward: never go to bed on an argument. It hadn't seemed much at the time but Mr Wigg had found it to be most important. He had said the same to his son before he married.

His mother's advice had been more cryptic, taking him half a lifetime to figure out. 'Don't forget she's her own person, son. She had a whole life before she met you.' It would have been much more helpful if she had said, 'Don't let her stop playing tennis', his young mind needing most things spelled out in plain language. He sometimes wondered, now, what his mother had given up, and who she had been before she became a wife and mother.

Jack, their gardener, had also offered plenty of advice. 'Women,' he said, 'are more complicated than they seem. And marriage, well, it's like trying to espalier a stone fruit. Two different stone fruit.'

Mr Wigg had coughed, unsure where it was all heading.

'It's like any other growing, it takes a lot of work, but you get back what you put in, son.'

They had built a garden of their marriage, a life. No one had much advice when it was gone, though, nor could they help you with the pain. It just had to be borne, like a terrible winter, or drought. One that didn't ever end.

# Coming Together

M̲r Wigg carried the pieces of the peach tree out to the shed one by one. Rats scurried off, unused to so much noise and daylight. It was time to start putting the tree together and there was not enough room in the workshop. He packed the leaves in one box and the fruit in another, carrying one under each arm, like a grocer.

It was overcast again, looking as if it might shower.

He wheeled out the oxy and latched the shed door open so it could not blow closed. He would weld the branches to the base, then the leaves to the branches, from underneath in most cases, and finally, attach the fruit. He had decided to use a link of chain so they would hang nicely, and, as his son had suggested, not get stolen.

Each large branch had a lug that fitted into a slot in the base, which he had only to oxy over to secure. The smaller branches were harder going. He tried to weld on the curve and to be as tidy as possible but his arms were quick to tire. Still, he was happy with the shape – not as open in the centre as a fruit tree should be, but pleasing to the eye.

He stood back to inspect his work once the first few leaves were attached. It would never be mistaken for a real tree, except perhaps at night, but it looked pretty good. It was taller than he had ever allowed any of his peaches to grow but he'd tried for the right scale for the village square, even though it would probably end up in his own garden. Or the chook yard, perhaps.

He worked on the lower section first, to get all the bending over and done with. He couldn't resist attaching a peach, to see how it looked. Mr Wigg smiled. Even the Orchard Queen would be pleased.

The light was going, or he might have been tempted to keep on until he was finished. Mr Wigg took one last look at his peach tree and wrestled the door shut.

Mr Wigg had been dancing. Just around the kitchen in his socks, while his dinner cooked, but dancing all the same. He had been remembering all the dances he and Mrs Wigg went to while still young, drinking punch and twirling around with their friends under the sparkling lights. He still knew most of the steps, though he was not as nimble on his feet as had once been.

They went less often as the years passed but they always made a fuss of it, Mrs Wigg buying a new dress and shoes and him a shirt and tie. Tucking one rose from the garden in his pinhole and attaching another to her dress as a corsage. One year she wore a watermelon-coloured organza gown and he managed to find a tie to match. They had danced together till midnight, around and around, until the band stopped playing. She had shimmered like a fairy queen and he had imagined their whole lives would play out like a fairytale, too. Forever and ever.

All of his wife's dresses were still in the wardrobe, including the watermelon one. He sometimes sat in there matching dresses to balls, or weddings and engagements. He knew he should deal with them, give them away, and not leave them for his son to sort out, but he didn't have the heart.

He turned the vegetables and spooned cooking juices over the lamb. Refilled his wine glass, to the top this time, and sat at the table to get back his breath.

The Orchard Queen lived an unnaturally long life. Fruit, it appeared, was beneficial to one's health, although perhaps not in the quantities she tended to consume it.

She called her gardener to her chamber, which she now rarely left. It was several hours before he appeared; he had taken to walking the wooded hills in the mornings, and the orchards in the afternoons, and moved more slowly these days. But when he arrived, he carried two white peaches from the Peach King in his wrinkled hands, as she knew he would.

The queen's gardener bowed and offered her the fruit.

The queen smiled, forgetting her rotten teeth. 'We have grown old, gardener,' she said.

The queen's gardener nodded. 'The fire in my hearth splutters, Majesty. It is time to choose another head gardener.'

The Orchard Queen cut a slice of peach with a dainty silver knife and placed it on her tongue. 'Ah.' She closed her eyes. 'The men you have suggested are very skilled. But they do not have your gifts.'

The queen's gardener sighed. 'No, Majesty.'

The Orchard Queen cut another slice of peach and held it out to the gardener, speared on the knife's tip.

The gardener took the slice and chewed slowly, letting the sweet juice trickle down his throat.

'You have served my husband and I very well,' she said.

'It has never been a duty, Majesty.'

The Orchard Queen smiled, and popped another slice, larger this time, into her mouth. 'Do you think it is the flesh of my husband that has given us so many years?' She held out a fresh slice, one painted eyebrow high on her white forehead.

The queen's gardener took the slice, examined its texture. 'Magic always has unexpected consequences, Majesty.'

'Good and bad, I suppose.'

'Indeed.'

Her chins wobbled as she chewed.

The queen's gardener looked past her, through the arched window, to the orchards. When the Orchard King had been carried home with an arrow through his throat, the queen – young, slender and beautiful in those days – had wept all over his face and wound, enough to wash away the dirt and blood. 'Do not leave me,' she had begged.

The gardener, then not much older than the queen and too soft-hearted, had backed out of the room and hurried away to fetch the smith. They whispered and worked in secret, with molten metal and the oil from plants, deep in the bowels of the castle, until the rooster crowed.

At dawn, the gardener had crept back into the king's chamber. The arrow had been removed but still he bled. The queen slept, her head on her lover's chest. The gardener put the vial to the king's lips and poured, saving the last drops for the wound itself.

The queen woke to find him there, holding the empty vial, and opened her mouth as if to call for her guards. Then the king opened his eyes, which had turned a swirling dark green.

They could not save him. The gardener's magic was only gentle, better suited to guiding plants and coaxing fruit, and the smith's powers usually channelled into swords and chainmail. But the king was able to say goodbye to his queen and ask to be lain on top of the hill in the orchard of white peaches.

At dusk on the third day, after the proper time for mourning, the king's body was lifted onto a pyre of walnut and elm branches, to which the gardener had added prunings from the peach orchard. The king's guard covered the pyre with oil, which the gardener had extracted from peach stone kernels. The band played the royal funeral song and the king burned into the night.

When the new day's light came creeping, the queen was staring out her chamber window, over her husband's still smoking funeral pyre, to the lands she now ruled. There was a shower of rain, as if from nowhere, illuminated by the sun's first low-angled shafts. Where her husband's body had lain, grown overnight, was a magnificent peach tree, its higher branches tangled together to form a crown.

And so the Orchard King lived on, as the King of Peaches, beneath the window of the queen. And she became ruler of the lands. Yet she would have no children, no heir. She took no lovers, it was said, loved only her fruit, particularly the flesh of one white peach.

'Neither you nor the smith had a son, gardener.' She handed him the last slice of peach. 'Will it all end with us?'

'I do have a daughter, Majesty,' he said. 'And she knows the ways.'

# Rose

As there were no aqua roses, his wife's favourite had been the Souvenir de la Malmaison. It was a pale pink double-bloom, the colour intensifying towards the middle, where the crowded petals looked a bit like a handful of tissues crumpled together. It had a kind of spicy fruit perfume, quite strong.

According to legend, the Empress Josephine gave the Souvenir de la Malmaison rose to Napoleon to bring him back safely from war. It was claimed to resemble Napoleon's hat, so was carried by French soldiers in the Battle of Waterloo to protect them. Napoleon survived his battles and died in bed, although Josephine was not by his side.

The rose had not protected Mrs Wigg from her battle with cancer. This was probably not surprising; although named after Josephine's gardens in Malmaison, near Paris, Souvenir de la Malmaison was actually developed in 1843, well after the reign of Napoleon, and the identity of the true 'Napoleon's rose' remains unknown. There were fifty-one varieties growing in his wife's garden but, evidently, none of them was the right one.

Mr Wigg was most fond of the Amoretto, a large apricot bloom with over a hundred petals and very fragrant. The Iceberg, bearing little resemblance to its lettuce namesake, was good, too, its white doubles blooming their heads off right into winter.

He walked, surrounded by roses, a mass of colour and perfume. He snipped a few, here and there, to fill a vase inside. Their thorns, as usual, did not care to prick him.

He tried to stroll through the garden every day when the roses were in season but it was nice to have some inside as well; as if his wife were still all around him.

Neither of them had helped his son prepare the place for sale; it had all been too difficult. And his wife was too sick by then, not wishing to be seen. His son was busy that month, but came down to fix the pump for the bore when it failed. He had a way with the thing. Though he always muttered and swore and said it needed replacing.

'What's wrong with Mum?' his son had said, frowning at the unweeded roses. 'She hasn't come out to say hello the last two times I've been.'

A crow settled in the shade of the shed door, cocked its head. Mr Wigg sighed.

'Is she still upset with me?'

'She is upset,' Mr Wigg had said. 'She's also unwell.'

He adjusted the shifting spanner with his thumb. 'What's wrong with her?'

'She has cancer, son.'

His son looked up. 'Since when?'

'We found out over summer. When you were on holidays.'

'And you're only telling me now?'

Mr Wigg lowered himself onto an upturned crate. 'There hasn't been a good time,' he said. 'With everything that's been going on.'

'Bloody hell, Dad! You didn't think it was relevant?'

'It didn't seem fair to add that to the mix,' he said. 'Your mother didn't want me to tell you.'

'Fair?' A breeze picked up outside, lifting an eddy of dust.

Mr Wigg watched the water dripping from the pump, pooling around its base bracket, which, now he noticed, was nearly rusted through.

'How bad?'

'It was in her breast. They tried to get it all but it's got into her stomach and liver.'

His son stood, squared his shoulders, as if it was something he could take on. 'They can treat it. Right?'

'There's nothing much more they can do,' he said. 'Except give her something for the pain.'

'Have you told Deb?'

Mr Wigg shook his head. Wiped the tears from his

cheeks. The crow took off with a mournful *awwww*, as if it was all too much.

'I'm sorry, Dad.' His son took a step towards him.

Mr Wigg got to his feet, gripped his son's forearms. 'It's not your fault,' he said. 'It's nobody's fault.'

# Assembly

Mr Wigg rushed through his breakfast and left the dishes in the sink. He let out the new chooks, still without names, throwing them their bucket of scraps from the kitchen to squabble over, and headed down to the shed.

It was a cool morning, a light shower of rain overnight before the cloud cover was whisked away. Perhaps the damp explained why he felt so ordinary, his limbs heavy and his thoughts slow. Like the fruit trees, he didn't respond well to sudden drops in temperature. Maybe he was just tired. He had lain awake under the clear sky, marvelling at the spangle of stars, his bedroom's semi-circle of windows like the cabin of a ship sailing the firth of night.

His hands were stiff and slow to work and he struggled with the latch on the shed doors. It was dark and cold inside. The mower looked at him reproachfully, left idle far too long.

He should have waited till later in the day to start work but the competition closed this week and his son was bringing Lachlan and Fiona over to see his tree tomorrow. He had promised to bring his camera, too, and photograph it properly.

Mr Wigg dragged the ladder out of the workshop and began attaching the leaves to the middle section. It was laborious going up and down, moving around a section at a time, and using the oxy at the top of the ladder was a bit tricky. He had only to glance at his tree to keep on, though. It was going to be magnificent, if he did say so himself. The more leaves he attached, the more it pleased him.

He took an early lunch, making a sandwich of leftover roast beef, chutney and cheese. He put the kettle on to boil while he ate. His wife's cup and saucer clattered as he put them down. He took out the little plate that went with them, too, for a piece of apricot pie. Since he was doing a hard day's work, he could afford to have a proper lunch.

The pie was good even cold, the juice from the apricots soaking into the pastry on the inside but still crunchy on the outside. He found himself wishing for his wife, to make her a cup of tea, too. She could be tempted by apricot pie, especially if he warmed a little slice for her and served it with a scoop of ice-cream. Mr Wigg blew his nose and wiped his face. His wife would have been impressed with his tree. Proud of him.

He piled all of his dishes into the sink, reached for a toothpick and his hat and stopped. His wife was reminding him he still hadn't rung his daughter. 'All right, all right.'

Mr Wigg set himself up at the phone desk in the hall and dialled the numbers with his little finger. There was no answer. They were all at work and school, of course. It had been a stupid time to ring.

He peered at the teledex. There was a recent work number, at the clinic. She wouldn't be able to talk properly, but perhaps his wife was right. This way he could give his daughter a chance to think about it. He turned the numbers, waiting for the dial to whir back each time.

A voice answered. Not his daughter's.

'Could I speak to Deb, please?'

'Can I ask who's calling?'

'It's her father.'

'Oh,' the voice said. 'She's just out at lunch. Can I get her to call you?'

'It's not urgent,' he said. 'When she gets home would be fine.'

'I'll let her know.'

'Thank you.' He put the phone down with a clatter. That was the best he could do for now.

The sun was warm on his face. The blue wrens were teaching their two young ones the ways of the world, hopping around the edge of the birdbaths. Every species had its own style of bathing; some reversed in, others threw themselves in headfirst. Some liked the water shallow, others deep. Robins fluffed themselves up into ridiculous featherballs. The wrens never lingered in the water long, lest they miss something, flitting their tails back and forth all the while.

The top section of the tree was much smaller but more fiddly, the closer branches making it difficult to get in behind each leaf. He'd had to prop the oxy right under the ladder, too, to reach. His hands were shaking badly today and his left arm ached. He had to take long breaks at times to have the control he needed for a neat weld.

At last, Mr Wigg smiled. All the leaves were in place. He took a drink of water from the tap and lay on the ground for a while to rest his back. The sky was as blue as he had ever seen it and a hawk circled above, watching for a mouse or rat careless enough to be sunning itself too long. Hopefully the little blue wrens' babies were tucked out of sight.

The leaves had settled onto his tree, as if they had always been part of it. It was a bit like the way you got used to a tree in winter, all bare. Then when its leaves returned, that seemed perfect, too. He breathed. It had seemed an impossible project some days, but he had done it! Almost.

He attached the peaches from the top first, so the job would get easier as he went. It reminded him of decorating a Christmas tree, hanging the most prized baubles, one third of the tree at a time. He moved the ladder around as he went and climbed back up for the last high peach.

The phone was ringing. The distorted sound from the speaker his son had put in the workshop finally registering. His daughter? He started to back down the ladder but his shoulder was giving him trouble. 'I'll never get there in time, love.'

A sharper pain ran down his arm and he had to stop to lean his wrist on the top step. He took a shaky breath. His wife was telling him to get down *right now*.

He tried to do as she asked but his legs wouldn't move. The real pain, when it came, was sudden and strong. Mr Wigg grabbed at his chest and fell backwards from the ladder, onto the ground. For a moment, he followed the path of a dandelion clock floating on the wind, and then it was gone.

# Epilogue

The summer of 1971–72 was a record season for stone fruit. Winter had given up plenty of frosty mornings, the spring rains had come late, and December and January had been hot and dry.

The Wizzy Wigg Fruit Dehydrator went into production in the first week of February. Department stores had been taking orders since Christmas and clearing off shelves in expectation of its arrival.

It was another mixed summer for cricket fans. Bradman selected a Rest of the World XI, captained by the great Gary Sobers, to tour Australia in place of South Africa. The world took a stand on apartheid, and Australia took on the world.

The public was slow to embrace the concept, in no rush to see history being made. Rubbish weather ended the Brisbane match in a draw. Then, in Perth, Lillee, unplayable on a rising pitch, took eight for twenty-nine in seven overs to dismiss the World XI for fifty-nine, and Australia won the match by an innings and eleven runs.

The Third Test was played in Melbourne, and this time the weather held and the crowds showed up. Sobers' two hundred and fifty-four runs with the bat and three for sixty-seven with the ball, were sobering indeed, ensuring a World XI victory.

In Sydney, Mr Wigg's son and little Lachlan, their esky on the empty seat between them, watched every ball bowled. A century from Ian Chappell was upstaged by younger brother Greg, who came close to a double, not out on a hundred and ninety-seven. Lachlan, with some encouragement from his father, waited for almost an hour to get their signatures on his new bat. Things were looking good for the Australians, before the weather intervened on the last day – another draw.

It all came down to the deciding Test in Adelaide, where the World XI handled the heat better to win by nine wickets and take the series. Despite fourteen centuries, a double century and one of the most remarkable bowling performances in history, the figures wouldn't count for the record books. The International Cricket Council, after a considerable delay, ruled that only matches in which a single country plays another were 'official'.

The morning of the annual Fruit Festival launch was a scorcher. The mayor sweated in his new suit, fidgeted with his collar. The crowd piled into the village green, waving festival programmes to fan their faces. Behind the mayor, his twin sons waited either side of a white-sheeted object twice their height, hands crossed in front of them.

'To announce the winner of the inaugural Sculpture Award,' the mayor said, 'I'd like to introduce one of our town's finest sons, Mr Tom Totner.' The crowd whistled and cheered. 'I'm sure you've all seen Tom on the box. Well, he's just off a plane from New York, where's he's been rehearsing for a new stage show that will tour the world.' The mayor turned, raised his hands. 'Will you all give him a warm welcome home.'

Tom bounced up to the microphone, flashed a Broadway smile. His looks had softened somewhat now, with age. Nonetheless, the women in the crowd let out a collective sigh, as if Totner was the one they had all let go, settling instead for their farmers and fruiterers. 'It's always a pleasure to be here for the festival. And you've really outdone yourselves this year,' he said. 'I'd like to congratulate Council on this wonderful new asset we're all enjoying today, the village green.'

The crowd cheered, forgetting all of their objections to the project, which had delayed the approval process to such an extent that the last trees had only been planted the night before, requiring spotlights and overtime.

Mrs Traubner took the camera from her husband, who, exhausted from the first week of vintage, was struggling to remove the lens cap. She stood high in her heels, determined to get a good photograph for Andy.

'It's my great pleasure to announce the winner of the Fruit Festival Sculpture Award.' He gestured towards the shrouded object behind him. 'Chosen from eighty-seven entries by our panel of Council and community members . . .' He ripped open an envelope, imagining himself, perhaps, waiting to go on stage at the Academy Awards. The mayor's sons stood to attention. 'The winner is . . . Mr Alneaus Wigg, for his work, "Peach Tree".'

He waited for the applause to subside. 'James Wigg will accept the award today on behalf of his father.'

Mr Wigg's son, stiff-backed and in the same suit he had worn to his father's funeral, stepped forward, shook Totner's hand, nodded and accepted the envelope.

'Could we ask you now, James, to do the honours and launch this year's festival.'

Mr Wigg's son cut the ribbon with the mayor's giant scissors. The boys pulled away the sheet with what was meant to be a dramatic flourish, but mistimed it. For a moment, white cotton flapped in the breeze then slipped down to one side. The tree shivered its limbs, stretched and adjusted its leaves. Its peaches gleamed. There was a collective *ooohhh* before the applause started.

Despite her mother's best attempt to grab her, Fiona pushed through the crowd and ran right past the mayor, pigtails flying, to throw her little arms about the Peach King.

# Acknowledgements

Thank you to Kate Eltham and the team behind the 2011 Queensland Writers Centre/Hachette Manuscript Development Program, for which *Mr Wigg* was shortlisted.

To Bernadette Foley, Kate Stevens, Daniel Pilkington, Chris Raine, Elizabeth Cowell, Ellie Exarchos, and the fabulous team at Hachette who have brought *Mr Wigg* to the world with such enthusiasm and grace – my warmest thanks.

Thanks to my fellow 2011 QWC/Hachette writers – Nicola Alter, Fiona Balint, Nicole Cody, Pamela Cook, Carolyn Daniels, Ross Davies, Susan Johnston and Alethea Kinsela – who have been wonderful company along the way, and a huge support.

I am grateful to Nike Sulway for her feedback on early drafts, and the wealth of insight and support given to my writing over the years.

A special thank you to my mother, Barbara Simpson, to whom this book is dedicated, for making it possible for me to put writing first in my life.

My grandfather, Jim Simpson, grew magnificent peaches. In many ways it is from his orchard that this book has grown.

# A note on fonts

The title design for *Mr Wigg* was created using letters from embossed gardening labels which were scanned, combined and manipulated in Photoshop CS6 to create a weathered, almost disintegrated effect that appears to be bleeding into the background. The exact typeface is unclear but it may be a variation of Apollo, which was designed by Adrian Frutiger in 1964, and has a wonderfully timeless and classic quality.

Inga Simpson began her career as a professional writer for government before gaining a PhD in creative writing. In 2011, she took part in the Queensland Writers Centre Manuscript Development Program and, as a result, Hachette Australia published *Mr Wigg*, her first novel, in 2013. Inga's second novel, *Nest*, was published in 2014, before being longlisted for the Miles Franklin Literary Award and the Stella Prize, and shortlisted for the ALS Gold Medal. The acclaimed *Where the Trees Were*, published in 2016, was Inga's third novel. Inga won the final Eric Rolls Prize for her nature writing and recently completed a second PhD, exploring the history of Australian nature writers. Inga's memoir about her love of Australian nature and life with trees, *Understory*, will be published in June 2017.

www.ingasimpson.com.au